Funderland

Nigel Jarrett is a freelance writer, a former newspaper reporter and a winner of the Rhys Davies Prize for short fiction. For many years he has been music critic of the *South Wales Argus*. Born in Cwmbran, he was educated at West Mon School, Pontypool, and Cardiff University. He reviews poetry for *Acumen* magazine and jazz for *Jazz Journal*. He likes drawing, never tires of gazing at his cat and lives in Monmouthshire with his wife, Ann, a former teacher.

Parthian
The Old Surgery
Napier Street
Cardigan
SA43 1ED

www.parthianbooks.co.uk

First published in 2011
© Nigel Jarrett
All Rights Reserved

ISBN 978-1-906998-51-6

Editor: Eluned Gramich

Cover design by marc@theundercard.co.uk
Cover photo by Getty Images
Typeset by books@lloydrobson.com
Printed and bound by Dinefwr Press, Llandybïe, Wales

Published with the financial support of the Welsh Books Council.

British Library Cataloguing in Publication Data

A cataloguing record for this book is available from the British
Library.

CONTENTS

For Ann

Funderland

While Carol was out, a gypsy woman came to the front door. Dale was walking from the kitchen to the bottom of the stairs when he noticed her standing there, the sunlight from behind shaping her silhouette.

It frightened him. He hadn't seen a gypsy since childhood and, like some phantom from way back, this one took a step across the threshold uninvited. Before he could protest, she offered him a lavender posy from a basket. 'How much?' he asked, slightly flummoxed and rummaging in his back pocket for change.

'A pound, sir,' she said. He took the flowers, gave her the coin and ushered her backwards. She was soon on her way.

Carol is downstairs, humming to herself and placing tins and jars on the kitchen table with audible thumps. Through the bedroom window and beyond the road, he can see a large bird, possibly a heron, stalled in flight against the wind, which is making an ocean of the meadow. Two months ago, huddled over the computer screen, they found the cottage on the internet. She laid a hand on his shoulder as he was scrolling the information, a nurse overdoing the comfort routine.

'Where are the flowers from?' she shouts up the stairs.

'A gypsy,' he calls back. 'Honestly. You must have passed her on the road.'

'Not I,' she says. 'Did she tell your fortune?'

He can remember when such a conversation with Rose would have bobbed on undercurrents of suspicion and distrust. But Rose is dead and her death has cleansed his memories of her. Of Johnny, too. Carol was always the odd one out, working a double shift when the three of them went to the seaside that time, just for a laugh.

'I thought we'd have tuna salad for lunch,' Carol announces when he comes downstairs with what is now just a faint limp. 'There's a brilliant little supermarket in the village. I got you a paper – the *Telegraph*. It's all they had.'

Again he hears the words coming from Rose, with their hint of reproof, the implication that she was the one who always had to choose, always had to discover the important things.

It is almost two years since the accident. He has vivid dreams. Rose and Johnny, brother and sister, are in the front seat as the car is ratcheted upwards through white timber thickets to the U-turn at the top of the ride. He is behind, watching the dripping water from underneath them as it flies off in the breeze like a necklace ripped from someone's throat. They had all been young teenagers when they last rode the dipper, but he remembered what would happen at the top, how the chain lifting them skywards would coil back on itself and send them freewheeling into the turning semi-circle, and how at the start of its unaided forward motion its nose would peck slightly to give it a boost before the full downward whoosh into the water. Except that this time, as it bore right, he felt the car being pulled from below, and to the accompaniment of splintering wood – he would always remember that sound – they began falling backwards, down through shattering spars and uprights until the car became wedged, somehow pinned by gravity, into a corner from where he could see Johnny and Rose plummeting like rag dolls to their deaths. There was a minor shift when the car dropped another six feet, as if Providence were trying to shake him free, but it came to nothing. Having been granted the best view, he was the leading witness at the inquest and the public inquiry. In a wheelchair, suffering a kind of shock-induced paralysis, he led the procession to the graves with Carol, Johnny's wife, at his side. As handfuls of soil thudded on the coffin lids and a breeze blew, he caught a whiff of her perfume.

They have been in close contact with each other since the accident. They have had lots to do, much weight to bear and no children to stifle any self-pity or be of practical help. They were together when the inquiry report absolving the fairground owners from blame arrived, and watched the TV item devoted to it. They had given no interviews. When the newsreader moved on to a piece about a factory strike, the whole episode seemed to close. Carol shared with other relatives the care Dale needed before he could walk again. After eighteen months the accident seemed like an event they had to forget because so many others had.

Renting the cottage was Carol's idea. Dale was tempted to raise the issue of what family and friends would think but resisted. They seemed to be all for it, as it turned out, perhaps because Carol was a nurse. She had told him at the inquest that they should always be available for each other. At the time, this sounded trite to him and he was glad to be able to reassure her whenever her guilt at being absent on the afternoon of the accident turned to tears, by convincing her that his own survival, hanging for all he was worth in agony up there where the wind cut into his face, often made him want to climb some other helter-skelter and throw himself off.

Carol is an inventive cook, the salad looking as though it took hours to prepare.

'Nice?' she asks, as he tucks in.

He nods approvingly with his mouth full. He can see on the worktop that she has also bought desserts: teaspoons balance on two flask-shaped cartons of something or other like the prelude to a ritual.

'Are you OK?' she asks.

He nods again and smiles. She reaches across and squeezes his hand.

'We ought to book if we are eating out tonight,' she says. 'There's that place down the road – or do you want to keep that till last?'

'We'll try it tonight,' he replies, and they look at each other, recognising the unspoken feeling they now share of something awful spoiling the run-up to a special occasion.

After lunch, Carol steps on to the patio in the garden to phone, sliding the French window behind her. She is standing with her back to him, laughing now and again as though she is making a personal call before speaking to the restaurant, something she forgot but hasn't told him about and wants to keep from him, but not too obviously.

From a distance, involved in a conversation that doesn't concern him, she appears different. The wind gets up and her free hand holds her skirt modestly in place at the back. But then it begins playing with her hair, which flutters uncontrollably. Dale knows that people are always saying that she is a beauty, and she is, but for a moment it has a strange revelatory quality for him, not to be suppressed. He notices the skirt, some flouncy, sky-blue material, and her lemon blouse, with its short puffball sleeves. All the commotion around her reminds him of something wild, in a wild place by the sea, but he puts this down to the memory of the gypsy woman and how it is colouring his imagination.

'Done,' she says, returning to the kitchen. 'No problem. Two seats for seven-thirty. A couple of hours. All we have to do now is take out a bank loan!'

He waits for her to explain that the chef or the person at the end of the line was a wag, but she adds nothing, except to say she is ready for a walk through the fields to the cove. There were two pictures of it on the PC screen when they booked, one obviously taken from the patio and the other from well down the path with the cottage imagined in the distance, like something in the process of receding completely from view, about to be lost for ever.

The description of the cottage as 'secluded' is accurate, because the building is old but appears marooned. A newly-whitewashed cube beside the sea yet backed by farmland, it has none of the paraphernalia – lobster pots, disused ploughs – associated with either. Dale wonders about its origins.

'Surf or turf?' he ponders after a while, as the field begins abandoning itself to the dunes.

'Oh – fish for me, I think, with a nice glass of crisp white wine,' she says.

He laughs: 'I meant the occupation of whoever lived here first, before people like us took holidays!'

Dale recalls how he and Rose saw the short-lived confusion when talking at cross-purposes in their early days as proof of a love so strong that it admitted no serious regression. But such a blissful state, he thinks, was so soon under threat because it was an accommodation, and being misunderstood became a fault of memory rather than a source of amusement, as it was now with Carol. When his feet begin treading the sand, he experiences one of the time lapses that the doctors have warned him about, a kind of stuttering of motion, as though there are several tenths-of-a-second that his brain, or a damaged part of it, has edited out in series. He feels like some extraterrestrial voyager in a sci-fi film, mechanically recording the alien scene in front of him. Just before it ends, Carol wanders into the frame from the left, like a stranger, a desirable earthling.

She pulls a face, seemingly stuck for an explanation of something, but before she can offer an opinion about the cottage's history, she turns to see a black dog bounding towards them. Beyond it, a woman is shouting at them or at the dog, it's not clear which. Then they catch a reassurance shredded by the wind, but a reassurance nevertheless, delivered in a posh, high-pitched voice – 'It's all right. She won't hurt you. She's a real softie. Don't worry!' Though the dog is not barking but wagging its tail as it draws closer, Carol faces it full square, both her arms outstretched, as if to protect Dale from what he knows she believes is an unpredictable breed. (Carol's sister, three years her junior, still bears a tiny scar on her nose where as an infant she was bitten by such a dog, a bull terrier.) The animal circles them twice before running off along the strand, its detour completed, while down beside the waves, its owner signals an apology before reaching for a piece of driftwood and throwing it for the dog to chase, away from them.

'Thanks,' Dale says, returning an extended scene to the level of intimacy.

'What for?' Carol asks. There is a slight edge to her voice, as if she has done something that has exposed a weakness.

'For saving me from the jaws of death,' he jokes, with a smile.

She picks up something herself, a shell, and playfully throws it at him. All the way to the water's edge, she walks apart, maintaining a distance. As the sand becomes wetter, she kicks off her flip-flops and hooks the straps over her finger. He moves behind her, still five or six yards away, watching her feet make momentarily dry prints that in seconds refill with watery sand. Unseen by her, he tries to step exactly where she has trodden. But she has a longer stride and bigger feet than his. She tips her sunglasses from the top of her head on to the bridge of her nose, like a visor, pushing them into place, and it is then that she stops and turns to face him. Though he cannot divine it, she is staring straight at him with something that might be concern or longing, her creased forehead robbed of meaning by her dark glasses, perhaps intentionally, and for the first time she links arms with him, not with any feeling of affection, for she does not draw him towards her or allow him to take any of her weight, but with an odd sort of purpose and a quickening of her pace, as though the white sound of the breakers, growing more deafening at their approach, is an ordeal through which he must pass with her help.

Between the headlands on either side of them, the horizon has grown less distinct. A faraway storm or a local, passing squall has erased its line, its razor-edge. But, within seconds, it is back, as clear as before, re-affirming itself. He has talked to her many times since the accident about memory being like this, gathering in the background, threatening to sweep inland and – yes – 'spoil' everything, all the progress. He has long been beached by its horrors and come to some sort of compromise, looking at it over his shoulder, watching it blacken the distance, and she has helped haul him to safety. But there have been return journeys, many walks to the sea's edge, since then, for confrontations with this nagging reminder which he couldn't have faced without her at his side, her grip tightening at every shudder of his fright and reluctance. Yet he knows this is not just a process, an exercise. He can only go through it because he wants her contact, the guilt of it always struggling against the hope that she feels the same way, that inside her there is something about her affectionate readiness to help him recover that is already being subverted by what is yet unspoken.

'What do you think they are thinking?' he asks. 'I mean, at this moment.'

'They?'

'You know – the others. Everyone.'

'I don't know.'

'Don't care?'

'Of course I care.'

She removes a wisp of hair that has drifted across her face. For a second, it seems to him like the act of someone who has been disheveled by exertion, an attempt to restore neatness and the appearance of order. He knows it has been hard for her, the one making amends for being protected by Fate from disaster and pain. At the same time, ahead of her probably, he reads it as something else, a response, not at all irritating, to some wind-borne harbinger of abandon, and he wants to stop strolling and embrace her, the passion of his intent enough to halt the incessant movement all around them: the slapping waves, the clouds, the woman and her dog (small figures now) disappearing into the dunes. They stop together, independently, and smile at their agreement.

'We'd better go back and get ready,' she says.

She showers first, standing in the bath with the moveable attachment. She is a few inches taller than he is, and when it's his turn, the drone of her hairdryer joining the sprinkling of water, he is able to stand beneath it. Her suds crowd the plughole, a remnant of her intimate presence. He bends painfully and scoops some of them on to his fingers.

There are two bedrooms, so low-ceilinged that they have to crane forwards to look through the seaview porthole of a window in each one. When they do they are brilliantly illuminated, as if from a spotlight trained on the building from outside. Sleeping arrangements were mentioned almost immediately after the holiday idea had been agreed. They joked about it but came to no conclusion. At the moment, Dale's clothes are hanging in the wardrobe in the room with the two singles, Carol's in the one along the tiny landing; both suitcases and odd scattered items are in that one too, on the double-bed, with its rose-printed coverlet. When the gipsy appeared, at first unknown to him, Dale was lying on one of the singles, staring vacantly at drifting clouds.

Strangely, only his room, the one he was lying in, also has the landward window, through which could be seen a distant mountain range and, closer, the stalled heron, or buzzard.

'I don't know what to wear,' Carol says from her room, the wardrobe door creaking. He imagines her pondering, lips puckered, finger rubbing the cleft of her chin, other hand on hip.

'I'm supposed to say that,' he replies, staring at the light, colourful clothes on their wire hangers, which tap their utility message against the back panel – clothes she helped him choose. 'Anything you wear will be right.'

For a few seconds there is silence, and he wonders if what he's said belongs to the class of endearments they now sometimes exchange, or if it is too bold an advance into more personal territory against which she is about to raise a barrier. But he smiles when she says, 'You flatterer, you!' As he is fingering the collar of a blue polo shirt, he can hear her dressing – the clack of heels on the wooden floor and a sound like paper crinkling. She takes a pink skirt and white cardigan out of the wardrobe, worried about the momentary lack of movement in his room, where he is standing still, his ears straining to catch her every intimate action. She hooks the clothes on the wardrobe door and lies back naked on the bed, knowing that he won't enter without knocking.

'Are you OK?' she calls, through the thin wall.

'Almost ready.'

She quickly dresses. 'Me too,' she says. 'Let's walk there – it's a nice evening.'

Though as physically restored as he'll ever be, he has to take stairs one step at a time. At the bottom, he waits for her. He hears her bedroom door click shut. Then there is an instant when there is no sound, no sign of her presence, as if she has been silently snatched away from him, and he feels beads of sweat forming on his temples. Then he looks up and she begins her descent. The old stairs are steep and for a second he can see her directly from below, her skirt billowing like a parachute, her long limbs glistening in the downstairs light, the rest of her in shadow. She is heavier than he is as well as taller and her weight, the weight of good health, makes the stairs creak, move even, as she grips the banister. He grows giddy, but then she is smiling, coming closer, holding out her hand for him. He grips it, as an anchorage for him and to help her dismount the rickety staircase, but he is too confused to separate need and chivalry and in his turmoil she keeps coming forwards, like a spectre in slow motion, and gently touches his lips with her own. As he places his hand on the side of her neck he can feel her heart, her good, good heart, pumping, and he catches again the graveside's feline perfume.

Doctor Fritz

It is late October. A Sahara sun has been baking the leaves in the spinney to a turn. He has detected a chill of late, inevitable but long-detained. It has not yet affected Tracey, the jolly little girl from the council who visits every few weeks, advancing towards him through the trees. The wireless speaks of creeping deserts and rising oceans, of coastlines crumbling into the sea. He has noticed that nothing will now remove the stain in the toilet (Kinsella, Belfast, 1936) and wonders if asking Tracey's advice will be interpreted back at her office as a further lowering of his guard. He guesses she has already told them of his asceticism, though that is probably neither an expression in her vocabulary nor, even if it is, something denoting conscious denial rather then negligence. She smiles whenever he stands at the portal of his incomprehensible world. He is sunlit, browned by a strange, meridional sun, while she is in shadow. He now thinks it was a mistake to tell her his name is really Fred, not Fritz. Dr Fred Stebbing, musicologist. It wasn't necessary. She has befriended him but her motives are ulterior. She is peeling away, manoeuvring him into a position of acknowledged helplessness. He looks to the *tshuapa* on the sideboard for anchorage. Although it has been explained to her, Tracey shows no interest in what lies behind it. Tracey accepts everything, takes notes. She is a simpering dossier-builder parting the branches, the branches that are refusing to surrender their leaves.

They do share common ground of a sort. Tracey sings in a band. He has seen her in the village in her stage gear, her out-of-work uniform: black leather mini-skirt; Dr Marten boots; and attenuated black T-shirt with random holes and tears, as though she has just been attacked by a panther. She wears dark lipstick and her eyes swim in deep pools of mascara, making her look like the Princess of Babylon portrait by Kees van Dongen. She brings with her to the cottage a clue to this other life, this afterlife, in the form of red streaks in her hair, but her idiot charm is their denial, and at first he was of a mind to draw her attention to it, as one might point out to an amateur actor, be it an insurance agent or a postman, that he had failed to remove all his make-up following an appearance in *Dear Octopus* the night before.

'I see you haven't washed up,' she says.

Her eyes are always elsewhere in the room, her pencil always doing cartwheels through her fingers. Sometimes her double life – pen-pushing busybody and Gothic *chanteuse* – irritates him.

'Why should I have?' he asks. 'It's only 11 o'clock.'

She looks at her watch, an object so large and unhelpful that it might have been designed as an aid to drowning an unwanted pet. Tracey comes from farming stock. Despite the magenta highlights, he sometimes feels that her interrogations represent some backwoods attempt to make a city-dweller justify his presence. Not that long ago, her mucky forebears would have taken a shotgun to a devoted but arthritic sheepdog and blown its head off. Maybe they still would. Still do. He whispers the word 'fey' and sings in a low, indistinct voice: 'Thro' they dash'd, and hew'd, and smash'd, till fey men died awa.' She hates that. Hates it when he's not normal. Continuing in a Scots accent, he leans forward and explains: 'Rabbie Burns.' She makes an appointment for the following month.

As darkness falls, he is dreaming. In his dream, he makes his way to the caves near the Quarra river. It is his first visit. One of the villagers has told him about the drawings. Deep inside what will become known as the Stebbing Complex, he places the lamp on a ledge, as directed by one of the Mompono elders. He chuckles in the half-light, as he always does when he thinks of old Mouyondze as an 'elder'; he barely comes up to his chest. Mouyondze's two grandchildren, who have tagged along, are, of course, the same height as ordinary children; it is only later that their growth will cease, like something stolen in the middle of the night and never missed. The water at their feet ripples, its movement translated into shadows on the damp walls. Then there is a grunt, and someone points a finger. As he lifts the lamp and holds it closer, he makes out the figure with the primitive *tshuapa*. Its two strings are unmistakable. The two-stringed *tshuapa*, confirmed before his eyes as ancient, played before words were written down, maybe before words were properly uttered. The soft undulations of the shadows are like accompaniments to the tinkling sounds of prehistory across the arc of time.

He tried to explain this discovery and its implications, not to mention the extent of his resulting prestige, to Tracey on her first visit.

'Very nice,' she said, turning the *tshuapa* in her hands, the faintest glow flickering on her cheeks from the polished facets of its belly – polished from use, he might have added, not upkeep. 'Can I have a go?'

'Yes, but pluck it gently. That's all it needs.'

She kept hold while he set the instrument in position. It was so small, almost a shelf ornament. He could tell from the way her left hand knowingly gripped the fingerboard that she had handled a guitar. But he didn't know then that she was a member of the strident Female Eunuchs. She vibrated the strings, singly and together. There were no frets and the wire was raised too far above the board for her to depress them without cutting her fingers.

'Ouch!' she cried. 'That's sharp.'

He waited for her to smile at the unintentional pun, but she just brought her fingertips to the end of her nose and scrutinised the thin bloodless valleys. The sound had meant nothing to her; was nothing, in fact. Not now. He recalled the irate Harvey Goldberger, whose researches had been eclipsed by the Quarra River finds. Perhaps Harvey had made a similar remark on reading the Transactions of the Congo Anthroposophic Society in September 1949, especially the piece by Dr Fritz Stebbing on Recent Explorations in the Riparian Caves of Eastern Mohjato. 'Ouch!' he might have said. 'That's sharp.' But that would have indicated a habit of resigned magnanimity to which tiny Harvey Goldberger, almost as small as Mouyondze, was eternally foreign. He was running too far ahead, almost as far as Harvey's revenge during the Mompono Ensemble's visit to the Festival of Britain in 1951. Some had said Professor Harvey Goldberger was miffed because of what had just happened to the Jews: professional ignominy following racial liquidation, the survivor winged by a stray bullet, as it were.

'Fred – did you or didn't you?' Tracey asked, replacing the *tshuapa* and taking up her notebook.

He stared at her for a few seconds, believing that the question prompted any number of answers from his half-forgotten past. 'Did or didn't do what?'

'Hold Mrs Anstey's cat under the drainpipe. She says it turned up looking streamlined, as though it had just flown home. Says at night she can hear you calling it Supersonic.' Tracey seemed to be reading this from written notes.

Florrie Anstey, a widow, is his neighbour. Their white-dipped cottages were once a pair at slightly different levels, built to house the blacksmith and gamekeeper of a large estate. They do not get on. It was Mrs Anstey who told social services of his self-neglect. Tracey on her first visit found there was some evidence for this in a raffish lifestyle. Then there was the signpost incident. He claimed Mrs Anstey's ire was provoked when he caught her deliberately vandalising a footpath sign – one of those post-mounted direction arrows bearing a white matchstick man on the move – which directed walkers through the woodland common to both their properties. He fell silent when Tracey questioned him about this because he realised that Florrie Anstey's desire for privacy and his advocacy of the exploratory instinct both had their merit, but the strange girl with black lips sitting opposite him beside a mug of undrinkable tea looked frightened by his gaze.

'I might have,' he replied cryptically, still staring. 'But then, this is rural Wales. Strange things happen around here.'

*

He is up early because he does not sleep well. The cat seems none the worse for its baptism. It responds to his whispered call – 'Soopersonic, Soopersonic' – as he sits outside in his cardigan, watching the sunrise above the hill opposite. He can hear a farmer whistling in sheep – B Flat, then a *glissando* to the double octave, two repeats and finally C capped by a staccato triplet on D Sharp. Down below, Florrie Anstey steps out of her front door as if in response to the shepherd, takes a long drag on a cigarette and returns inside, where she has lit a fire. Thick yellow smoke begins rising to the treetops from her chimney. They've had a disagreement about that, too. She will have no truck with storage-heaters, not even in the interests of the environment.

He wonders what Tracey is telling them back at the council office, wonders whether there is a file on him. Once, he received her unshaven in vest and trousers with his braces hanging loose. She told him he merged into his background, by which she meant leaning towers of washing-up, Manhattans of books and boxes, eroding mounds of papers, a pair of hedge-clippers, a steam iron and long-johns on the table, food half-eaten or untouched, dead and dying flowers and net curtains sagging on overstretched cord. 'It's that fucking witch down there,' he mumbled. 'She's put the hex on me.' But this time he has tidied up, put stray objects in drawers and opened the windows. It's like a spring day. He's even wearing a tie, though there are no clean shirts. Above the fireplace, presiding over his reluctant attempt at contrition, is a photograph of him in a white linen suit, flanked on each side by three pigmies, the Mompono Ensemble. The sun has turned the lenses of his wire spectacles into white discs and he is stooping slightly with his arms expanded, as if to minimise his height, his colour and his position as civilised broker or intermediary; the pigmies, wearing head feathers and holding thin spears, are not smiling. One of them clutches a barely visible *tshuapa*.

A car slows and stops on the bottom road. A door slams shut. Then he sees Tracey leaning into the steep flight of steps past Lower Clytha Cottage, her black overcoat trailing behind her. She is also wearing a Russian-style fur hat. If he had a rifle, he could halt her approaching malignancy with one pop, then fell the chain-smoking vandal as she wobbles out to investigate.

'And how are we today?' she asks.

'Is that the royal "we"?'

She looks mystified, so with a sigh he beckons her indoors.

On the table, beside other items, a stone, two vases and a teapot hold down an unfurled bill poster. She already knows about the Ensemble, the *tshuapa*, the cave drawings appearing out of the dark like photographs developing in a tilted tray, the immemorial drip, drip in the distance, the explorer and his retinue of little folk paddling in black water.

'Here we are, the Mompono Ensemble at Morley College, September, 1951,' he explains, tracing the letters on the poster with a forefinger, its nail capped by a neat crescent of grime. 'But you see' – he looks up rheumily at her from another epoch – 'one of them went missing.'

'What – one of the pigmies?'

'We were all staying in a hotel paid for by the Embassy and the British Council, off the beaten track a bit. In fact, Lambeth. Harvey Goldberger was there, with a few people from the CAS.'

Her brow furrows, but she lets him continue.

'It was Mouyondze's nephew who vanished, the evening after the second performance. They didn't know where they were. They moved together down the corridors, huddled, like a breakaway shoal of fish. I think he was frightened, or curious. He got out through a lavatory window no bigger than a postage stamp. They were fascinated by the toilets, so we indulged them.'

She starts to smile. It's more than that, because she tries to stifle it with her ring-encrusted fingers.

'But you found him.'

'They insisted on wearing their loincloths all the time, though we had supplied them with grey schoolboy jerseys. In those days, autumns were just brief overtures to winter. Not like now.'

As if to confirm this, the shadow of a moving branch makes merry on the whitewashed back wall.

He tells her that Harvey Goldberger never recovered from news of the Quarra River discoveries, explains how Harvey was a brilliant theorist with a speculative view of antiquity. He says he proved Harvey wrong in the most devastating and comprehensive fashion – empirically; not only had he renewed contact with the Mompono on the flimsiest reports of their existence but they had taken him into their confidence enough to vouchsafe a connection that meant nothing to them but which to him was breathtaking. He explains how Harvey grasped the opportunity to make mischief on the night of September 30, 1951 by alerting the newspapers to the disappearance, and why Harvey could not have wished for a better outcome: a *Daily Mail* reporter and photographer, turning into St Mary's Gardens, spied the shivering little fellow in his pullover; he was standing still, hypnotised by his lengthening shadow, his javelin tapping nervously on the spot like a blind man's stick.'

But before the end of his story, she is yawning. He is insulted by her boredom. Yet she is not like those who cannot help themselves but are redeemed for him in other ways – no, her ignorance, her lack of sympathy, is gleeful; she revels in it.

'Fred, you are almost ninety,' she informs him, as though awaking from a parallel thought-journey.

For a few seconds, her announcement wavers between reminder and admonition, and the delay allows her to proceed. She holds herself erect and clears her throat.

'Mrs Anstey saw you the other evening... well... coopying in the wood – and cleaning yourself with leaves.'

He offers no response to her pretence of approaching climax. Mention of the wood, the spinney, reminds him of the time he explained to her how his rotten family tree had been felled beneath him.

'She's lying,' he says, without feeling. 'There are no leaves to speak of. They're late this year. Or hasn't she noticed?' Close to her, he becomes aware of her thicker eye shadow and the more lurid dye in her hair. Painted for the kill – or the appearance of the Female Eunuchs that night at the Memorial Hall. Her metal hoop earrings are pendulous yet fixed in space, picking up no internal quiver of commiseration or remorse; he can see himself reflected in them, twins bent to a bow's shape. Her last words echo: 'I'll be back!'

*

He has heard the distant noise before, its turmoil spent in flashing lights above the edge of the village. This time, it begins at dusk, and now its element, the night, is settling all around. The dark will soon be complete, like a creek gorged by the incoming tide. He takes a billhook and a torch and descends into the spinney towards Lower Clytha Cottage. A radio at an open widow tells him that Florrie Anstey has been joined by a laughing, applauding concert party.

Then he sees it directly in front of him – a new footpath sign. He flicks on the torch and spies above his head a little lime-painted Mompono tribesman scurrying to the Quarra River caves, where the *tshuapa*-player, as thin as a reed, awaits his cue. And at last, accomplices of the dark and edged with frost, they begin to fall on his upturned face, leaf after leaf after leaf.

Watching the Birdie

They were approaching Porlock on the long coastal drive to St Ives. Kate's new dad had long talked about the place in that way he had of hooking a thumb in his waistcoat and holding his cigarette away from him in his other hand as though close up it might do him an injury. Her stepbrother, Max, was with her in the back, his wiry ginger hair rippling in the breeze from the driver's open window.

'Do you think she'll make it, Max?' Mr Charlton asked, meaning Porlock Hill.

Mr Charlton always referred to cars as 'she'. Boats too. 'She's a beauty!' he'd said, on that day they saw the paddle-steamer churning up river before taking them across the Channel to Ilfracombe, when the colour of the water changed from brown to bottle-green like one of Miss Moseley's experiments in Year Six.

He addressed many of his questions to Max, as if she and her mother were not there, but whenever she complained about this she was told to be patient – it was bound to be awkward at the start.

Max ventured no opinion on the ability of their Standard Eight to lift itself out of Porlock on to the moor. At one point, while turning a sharp bend, they seemed to be staring through the windscreen straight at the sky. Whatever the weather, Max's nose was always bubbled with sweat. When Kate wasn't looking directly at him, he sneaked glances at her. This she could see out of the corner of her eye, and she hated it.

The boat trip, the fortnight in Cornwall and other 'treats' were new. They'd never had a car when her father was alive and no money for days out in the 'Waverley', with its sleek pistons below deck, watched over by boys on tiptoe and men sucking pipes. She'd been with her father when he died, when his eyes went white and he'd fallen in a heap before her on the back lawn. She had felt the ground shake. Mr Charlton had told her that to have been there when it happened was a privilege she would learn to cherish, but when he'd said this she saw her mother looking at him and shaking her head.

Nevertheless, Kate liked Mr Charlton. One afternoon, they'd driven to Cheddar Gorge for a picnic, and he'd laid a little check tablecloth on a ledge high above the road. She'd heard her mother whispering that it was making her giddy, up there where people were looking at them from below, shielding their eyes from the sun. But Mr Charlton had made the danger disappear by holding the cloth at two corners and shaking it so that it floated to a perfect square on the grass, like a parachute in slow motion. She'd liked the way he'd looked around him and smiled, as if seeking applause.

Now that they were on the flat, with the sea to the right, Mr Charlton began to sing. She wanted to join in but she didn't know the words. Her mother had a go at the choruses.

'How are we doing, Max?' Mr Charlton asked, his face looking at her in the rear-view mirror. Max had few answers to his father's questions and none were expected.

'All right, Mrs Charlton?' he inquired, leaning towards her mother, who was next to him in her flower-printed frock and red beret. 'Not too hot?'

Kate could not understand why her mother looked so unhappy. Was it about being a widow for too short a time, or producing a new father out of a hat? She'd said there would be a lot to get used to in marrying Evan Charlton, the Betterware man. Each day he left for work early and arrived home late, and on weekends he organised 'excursions' and made lists of things to do. Her mother had even asked if she minded, as if anything Kate said could have made her act differently. At the Dancers Club, they'd had a draw one night for single members and the names of Esme Bright and Evan Charlton had been pulled out of the hat for the foxtrot. They'd had to dance alone for three minutes in a moving pool of light, because it was the rule. Soon after, her mother had brought Mr Charlton home. Even then, he had a surprise for her – a three-link chain in chromium steel, the idea being to separate the links. Before she could try it herself, he had done it for her, quickly, so that she couldn't follow. Then he'd put the links back again with one hand and jangled the completed chain before her face, like a hypnotist. That evening, Max had stayed with one of his aunties. Soon after, they'd gone to the Charltons' house, a big place on the edge of town that echoed and always felt cold. It had coloured glass in the front door and a porch with an iron 'H' for scraping mud off shoes. His wife, Max's mother, had still been alive, divorced, but there were no pictures of her. For a while, as they'd stood in the hallway, Max had watched them from the landing.

'Looks like a good place for a stop, Max,' Mr Charlton said. 'Everyone in favour say Aye.' They all said 'Aye!' and the car pulled on to a patch of ground by a five-bar gate. When they were seated, Mr Charlton said 'Watch!' and produced six lumps of sugar from his right shirt sleeve.

'How did you do that?' Kate laughed, squatting on the blanket her mother had fetched from the boot, along with a Thermos flask from under the dashboard.

'He put them up there when you weren't looking, stupid,' Max said.

'Max, don't be so nasty to your sister,' Mr Charlton said. 'We're on holiday.'

'Does that mean it's all right at any other time?' Kate's mother asked, letting the words slip out under her breath.

'Now look what you've done,' Mr Charlton said. 'You've upset your mother.'

'She's not my mother,' snapped Max, turning his gaze on Kate. 'And she's not my sister.'

'Gosh, we are in a tiz, today,' said Mr Charlton. 'Aren't they, Kate?'

Mr Charlton decided that they would break their journey at Barnstaple. Kate heard them discussing it after he had booked their St Ives B&B. He'd told her mother he had the money. Max, in a better mood, announced that they stopped over before because it was a long journey: twelve hours, especially if the Beachley-Aust ferry was busy, which it had been, with all those cars on the slipway dipping towards the water and their drivers gazing at the estuary's glitter. Mr

Charlton only used the crossing for holidays. At other times, his car stacked with polish, mops and cylinders of Vim, he would take the long route through Gloucester. One evening, with her mother knitting by the fire and Max fiddling with his Meccano, he'd shown Kate his itinerary for the following day, a Friday, and his list of orders in places she'd never heard of – Aylburton, Minsterworth, Dursley, Easter Compton. Drawing close to her, he'd said: 'I want you to be at the front door when I get home at six.' She'd caught Max turning to her with a surly expression. She'd done what her stepfather had asked, to find that he'd returned with more than his outward stock. But her glee had been forced because Max had already told her that every weekend at a depot in Bristol his father would replenish the wares he kept piled in the spare bedroom. Because she hadn't let on, she felt Max taking a step closer to her, and she'd somehow feared keeping her knowledge from his father, her stepfather.

'Let's be having you all,' Mr Charlton said when they'd finished, tapping the end of another cigarette on the lid of his silver case. His cigarette fingers had iodine stains on them, which turned a buttercup yellow after scrubbing but never went away. He had shown her once.

Max was already sitting in the car. She saw her mother struggle to her feet.

'Are you all right, mam?' she asked.

'Just a bit of tummy ache, love,' her mother said as she got up in two goes, weightlifter fashion. Her stepfather didn't notice because he was reading a road map with his back to her and peering into the distance.

'Do you know, Max, we've travelled this way many times but I'm never sure of the turn,' he said. When he gulped in smoke it stayed inside him for ages until he decided to let it go, dragonlike, through his nose. Max watched Kate and her mother approaching the car. He gave them another of his gruff looks, which made Kate feel that he regarded them as two hitchhikers they'd regretfully picked up.

But when they were chugging along again and Mr and Mrs Charlton were speaking to each other in the front – sharing a joke, in fact, because Kate saw her mother turn her head away and blush secretly – Max became friendlier.

'He always gets lost about here,' Max confided in a whisper. 'It's all because he likes whizzing along country roads. One summer we ended up in Woolacombe. He told mum he meant to go there, to show us the long beach. After that, if he did something he didn't mean to, mum called it 'a Woolacombe'. Like the time he put weed killer on the lawn and killed the grass. He said he did it to start again, to make a proper lawn instead of the scraggy one we had. A Woolacombe, mum said.'

Kate didn't like Max. He smelled like a dog smells when it has been out in the wet and his legs appeared to grow longer each day. His hands were always moving in his pockets, like Bobby Berridge's had been that time he smuggled a white mouse into class. She was glad when Mr Charlton caught her attention again in the rear view mirror. With his thumb and finger he pretended to pluck out his left eye, buff it on his lapel and replace it – the wrong way, because he was cross-eyed. So he repeated the trick and got it right.

When he saw Kate's face light up, Max sneered and stared fixedly at the back of his father's head, where Brylcreem had made teeth of his plastered hair. 'It's Brylcreem that makes your collars dirty,' his mother had once said. They'd always argued. When she'd left, in a grey suit and smelling of rosewater, she'd knelt down with tears in her eyes and hugged him. If only his father had known where things were – collars, studs, the road to Barnstaple with Arlington Court sailing by in the distance – she might have been in the front instead of that stupid woman in her stupid beret, and he'd have been in the back alone rather than with the person who might have been his girlfriend if she hadn't been his step-sister. He suddenly felt hungry.

'Not long now, Max,' Mr Charlton said, checking that it was Kate who was reassured.

Because they'd had to wait for the ferry, it was approaching dusk when Barnstaple appeared in the distance. They passed a fairground with anguished, riderless horses rising and falling on a carousel, and began driving slowly down a back street of guest houses. In the lighted windows of some, old people were silently eating.

'There it is: Pilot House,' said Mrs Charlton. 'Doesn't look as if there's anyone in.'

'Don't fret, Ez,' Mr Charlton said. 'It's all booked.'

Kate's father had never called her mother 'Ez'. But he also couldn't have told you what card you'd picked from a shuffled pack or where a button was hidden under a row of three shifting thimbles. 'Ez' was something new, and at everything new, Kate's mother turned to her daughter, lifted her shoulders and looked helpless.

The sight of Max eating made Kate retch. It wasn't so much eating as noisy shovelling. The landlady, dressed as if to go out, was what Kate's father would have called 'hoity-toity'. She served them herself, telling Mr Charlton that her 'girl' had gone home and implying that her attentions were therefore a privilege, though Kate thought her turned-up nose might also have been a reaction to Max's behaviour at the trough.

'Max appears to be famished, Kate,' Mr Charlton said, by way of excusing his son's antics. Then he looked at her mother. 'You'll have to sort him out, Ez. It'll be one of your jobs.'

Max was so tired that his eyes were closing and his head was dropping on to his chest, movements punctuated regularly by sleepy, bemused revivals.

'It's up the stairs to Bedfordshire for you, young man,' Mr Charlton said, rising to his feet like someone who had decided that his patience was exhausted but winking at Kate to suggest that she was beyond his imperative.

It was then that Kate saw her mother move to Max's side and begin running a hand through his hair, which on their journey had been unravelling and was now out of control. Sometimes, like now, the blobs of sweat on Max's nose ran together and flowed to the end of it.

'Come on, Max,' she said. 'You must be dog tired.'

Kate's impulse to snigger was stifled by the hint of abandonment in her mother's action, which seemed to ignore her despite her own tiredness. It was then that she felt Mr Charlton's arm sliding across the back of her chair and coming to rest on her shoulders, and she recalled the way Miss Moseley divided up the class into groups for reading with a pointed finger but not saying a word, the best with the best and the rest with one another.

'We'd better sort out the rooms,' Mr Charlton said, though he had already placed the big suitcase in the double with the rose-pattern wallpaper and Max's duffle-bag in the one next to it, reached through a connecting door.

'You come, too,' Kate's mother told her. 'I'll get your stuff.'

Kate's 'stuff' comprised soap, flannel, scrubbing-brush, a limp stick of emery board and the things she knew she would now need every few weeks until she was an old woman. Her mother had told her so. Though associated with pain, she was pleased to have taken charge of something of which the stupid Max would only ever have an inkling. It was therefore her mother who led her to the attic room once Max, lying like a rag doll on the quilt, had been stripped to his vest and pants and been tucked in.

Kate's room had no window and belonged in a dream. It was as high as you could go in the house. The sloping roof meant there was no ceiling. It scared her. She thought she might wake in the morning to find it had grown smaller, and this made her feel hot. She was undressed and in her nightie when her mother entered, clasped her silently and whispered, 'Goodnight, sweetheart' with a kiss on the forehead and a lingering look that seemed to say, 'Perk up, old girl; everything will be all right!'

As the new Mrs Charlton left, Kate could see Mr Charlton waiting his turn at the top of the stairs in the half-light, the bit of the stairs that had been added on like part of a doll's house and which clattered when her mother came up before descending to the carpeted landing.

'Is this OK, princess?' her stepfather asked, closing the door behind him and gently snapping it shut. He spoke quietly. She could barely hear him. He seemed taller in the little room.

She nodded, remembering that her father had often called her that, especially when he wanted her co-operation – if he'd been too tired to take her to Brownies, for instance.

She was sitting on the side of the bed with sheets pulled back and her mother's new husband was standing before her. She was afraid his eyes might roll and that he would fall with a thump on the floor and make the landlady angry. He seemed to fill her little space in the sky. She couldn't see his face properly because he was beyond the light shed by the bedside lamp, but he looked strange, in the way grown-ups do when they have been let down.

Then she started as he shot out his right hand into the lamplight. The fingers were straight but closed together, all except the forefinger, which was missing its top two joints. He took a step forwards and brought up his left hand, with the top joint of its thumb missing and its forefinger resting on the stump. Next, he placed the left thumb beside the shortened right finger and, with the join covered, moved the top of the left thumb up and down as though the broken right forefinger were in two pieces.

She giggled and put her wrist to her mouth, but immediately he spread both his hands to reassure her ('Don't get the girl too excited,' she'd heard her mother say) and he, too, sitting himself beside her, chuckled, raising his knees and slapping them.

But that was the moment it fell into the bowl made between her legs by the nightie – the top of a finger, pink and covered in blood where it has been sliced off, yet making no stain, no mess, and she felt tears rising and saw objects splintering in the light.

He drew closer. 'Don't worry, princess,' he said. 'That's

the joke, you see. Not the trick with the hands but where I've hidden the bit of plastic finger. Did you guess it was plastic? Do you know where I'd hidden it?'

She didn't know how to answer, what to answer, and as her fear fought the giggles, his hand, his uninjured right hand and its buttercup-stained finger, moved towards the bowl in a slow, hushed act of retrieval.

Nomad

My father should have seen me at first, feeling sorry for myself when I ought to have been a bit more imaginative. 'Take a grip of the situation,' he would have told me. But I was upset. The start of that whole business with Mick made me physically ill, and not just because of a sense of loss or failure. It's hard to explain how I've just about got over it late in the day. Maybe I caught a glimpse of a hidden self.

Molly and I used to look forward to the time when we would finally be on our own. The whole place to ourselves. No dependants under the same roof, a feeling of paid-for freedom. Even the cat was part of the scheme, its death the end of a relationship that nothing could replace. Everything would go as planned, leaving only the two of us. We all need time to look at life, to examine our lives, and decide what's in and what should be out, done with. And others may have to make sacrifices to ensure we can do so.

Perhaps it was a mistake to move into this house, the one Molly's great-grandfather built. There are four of them, identical but discreetly separated, on the road out of town, and in their way they still look quite modern. Molly's Uncle Max lived here before us but he had to be shifted into a nursing-home – he's still there, hanging on – so we bought it from him, partly to provide him with funds. Error or not, I have come to love our house. The architect, a friend of Molly's great-grandfather, went mad, threw himself out of a high window, his long moustache swept back like a swallow's wings. I think there must be a lot of him in the design, a lot of the superfluous stuff, off the point, enclosing a solid core. I once read a piece about Bell, the inventor of the telephone: it appears that, in his dotage, he thought a massive block of ice might be raised by the condensation coming off it, like a hovercraft. I suppose it was a case of genius run to seed. Anyway, in this house there is a long landing with recesses and plaster gargoyles, and at the end a circular window of stained glass.

At the time, I was selling insurance and Molly had been working for three years as a nursery assistant. Pensions were the coming thing; I was being trained to go out and tell people how flawed their pension arrangements were – that was if they had made any at all. It was true: people never think of the future. For once I felt I was being paid for doing something worthwhile. Molly seemed happy, though Mick, our teenage son, was becoming a handful. One night he arrived home skewingly drunk, bundled out of a taxi on to the drive. We overlooked it, put it down to an overstretched adolescence. Then, one afternoon when she was with her kids on a trip to a nearby town, Molly saw Mick, who should have been at school, walking in the park with an old man – older than me, at any rate. The man had his arm around Mick's shoulders. I smiled inwardly when Molly told me she'd had to divert her crocodile of little charges. She was certain it had been Mick – well, almost.

Strange as it may seem, we couldn't bring ourselves to tackle Mick about it, not even the truancy part. He'd never gone absent from school before. In fact, he was bright and attentive in class. But things got worse. One weekend, Mick ran away, leaving a note. We received a picture postcard from London. It showed a woman smothered by pigeons at the foot of Nelson's Column. She was feeding the birds, this woman, yet seemed to be in some kind of private torment, while all around her laughed or strolled idly by.

Neither of our other two had ever been difficult. Peter, the oldest, is a teacher in London, which raised our hopes for Mick when the boy began to give us grief. Settled down – that's the expression we all use to describe the time after we've taken hold of our lives. Peter was settled. Maria, too, our middle one: she was married to Jed, a trainee supermarket manager, and they were about to make us grandparents. You could say we'd been model guardians. Not that we'd tried; we'd just done what we'd thought was best by our children and had hoped things would turn out pretty well.

On the Saturday Mick left, we went over to the house Maria and Jed had bought. Jed was fitting kitchen units and decorating. Unlike me, he's very practical. I remember his cheek was smudged with paint, like a lipstick heart, when he came into the living-room.

'That boy needs a kick in the trousers,' Jed said of Mick. (We'd sorted out straight talking as well, though its unguarded expression often gives me a jolt.)

'You must feel terrible,' Maria said. She'd already referred to her younger brother as a tearaway. She was wearing one of those dungaree outfits specially shaped for mothers-to-be. She was carrying all before her.

Molly was exasperated.

'It's not us!' she stammered. 'It's him we're worried about.'

But Jed was unmoved. He shook his head at the pair of us, Molly and me, and just for a moment I understood why so many people spurn the pity of others. It must make them feel small. We didn't need moralising from Jed; we wanted him as someone not much older than Mick to offer an explanation for his behaviour.

Back home later the same evening, we phoned Peter. He had been out in the day and now he was halfway through marking. I could hear a jazz record playing and other voices in the background. I didn't ask if he had company and he didn't mention it. I quite like that. It's evidence of another life going on independently of your own, with small private happenings that have nothing to do with you even though you are conscious of them.

'Well, he hasn't contacted me,' Peter said, a bit matter-of-factly. 'What's the postmark?'

I told him 'N15' and there was a pause as we both must have admitted to ourselves that this represented the proverbial haystack. I sustained a vision of endless streets, and a vast swarm of the desperate and dislocated.

'He can look after himself,' Peter said, cheeringly. 'He's not dull. Perhaps he'll contact me. I hope he will. Perhaps there are things he needs to sort out.'

I think Peter silently acknowledged my equally tacit recognition of the hint of exclusion in this last remark. Molly was hovering at my shoulder. As if catching it too, she signalled me to hand her the receiver.

'Why couldn't he have discussed it with us?' she asked. 'There's nothing wrong – nothing.'

She stared at the wall, then handed Peter back to me, her fellow conspirator.

'There was a bit of bother a while ago,' I explained. 'Or so we think.'

He listened without interrupting as I told him about the incident in the park. I think it was knowing that he was not alone in ignorance of the facts that he remained calm – a case of parents still exercising their right to information, no matter how old their children.

'I'll do what I can,' he said. 'The police up here might be able to help. But don't forget that he's gone of his own accord. They usually aren't interested.'

I somehow felt that he was speaking from a kind of wearisome experience. He tells us horrendous tales of school-mastering in the slums.

When we sat down, Molly and I, it was obvious that she had expected more from Peter, such as an immediate tour of north London with his jazz-loving friends. I couldn't see it myself. I thought instead of Peter gazing briefly out of the window, telling his pals about a rebellious brother, then palming another exercise book from the unmarked pile. I don't know why I thought this. With independence, some things have to be taken for granted. A certain coolness prevails, encouraged by distance, other worlds, the very stuff of striking out on your own from where those who have nurtured you come to terms with the difference between love and the memory of love. I couldn't help considering that

37

snipping the apron-strings, as one must, leaves one totally lacking control, that studiously avoiding overbearance in life turns loved ones into, albeit favourable, strangers.

Molly and I saw to it that Jed, Maria and Peter would be there when Mick arrived home for the first time. We all managed to mask our different feelings about what had happened. It wasn't exactly the best arrangement for discovering why Mick had run off. He seemed, outwardly at least, well-adjusted, if a little downcast at the anxiety he had caused. I got the impression that, in some odd way, Mick had done the right thing. Chastising is almost foreign to me and Molly; it's just the way we are.

'If there's anything we can do, just say,' Molly told him when she cornered him alone in the house on that half-celebratory weekend. But little any of us said actually sounded as if it connected with what he must have been feeling inside. Then he left again, without ceremony and almost without warning, before we had embarked on a long discussion. Maybe the threat of an ensnaring adult superiority was what made him go.

I wouldn't say Molly lost interest in Mick's wanderings from then on, because the rest of the family also grew resigned to his peculiarity, if that's the word. We kept the postcards. Within Molly and Jed there developed an unspoken indignation, which I think they found supportive. I have always been uncomfortable about taking unwarranted offence. Of course, I pitied Molly in the place where she was exposed as uncomprehending. Just before events took their surprising turn, I began trying to make sense of what was happening. For a start, I understood how difficult it is for us to communicate the predicament of a third party to others.

When I recall Molly's story of seeing Mick in the park with his mysterious comforter, it is the image which persists, inviting surmise, and there are moments when I would prefer this evocation to be all there is, like the picture I retain from my father's testimony of my uncle (a boy then, later to die of rheumatic fever) sprinting bare-chested like a lunatic around my unemployed grandfather's allotment, his shirt billowing behind him as dusk and dampness infiltrated their sustaining half-acre; it was in the Depression, that dewy antithesis of joy and innocence.

I was at home nursing a cold the day Mick's airmail letter from Marrakesh arrived. I saw it float towards the doormat as I was going downstairs to make myself breakfast. It was addressed to me. Its thin, blue paper belied the visual gravity of its contents, which, on being unfolded, seemed to demand to be read aloud. 'Dear dad', it began, 'As I write this, the imam is calling the faithful to prayer...' The rest was nothing less than a story, a fascinating story. I imagined Mick in a white, loose-fitting garment, exuding the confidence of one totally assimilated by place. He shares a home with others, by the sea. The tall palms bend a little before the on-shore winds. There is trouble with Allal, the gardener. Allal is trying to get his boyfriend moved into the house, which is owned by a Frenchman with a pointed beard. But the Frenchman won't allow it on the grounds that Allal will want to live in, too, and thus neglect his duties, which involve keeping the grounds tidy for prospective buyers – the house is always up for sale but the Frenchman is a laconic vendor. It is Mick's problem because the Frenchman has appointed him unofficial custodian in his absence. One of Mick's jobs is to see that Allal turns up on time and completes his allotted hours. Mick has clearly risen in some loose hierachy, some distant confederation of the languid. Instead of wondering what Mick was thinking of in sending such a disarming, guilt-free missive from that house beside the sea, I tasted brine on my tongue and began to worry about overgrown funerary urns. When Molly arrived home from the nursery, I betrayed what might have been an expected confidence by telling her about the letter. She shook her head while reading it.

When I told Jed and Maria, I merely indicated that we had received a message from Morocco to say that Mick was well. This seemed to satisfy them, though perhaps I interpreted satisfaction as lack of curiosity. Peter's greater inquisitiveness never exactly pinions you, but I knew that holding nothing back would pre-empt further questioning. Then a second letter arrived, and a third, each addressed to me. Molly took no offence at this partiality; she was glad I had pocketed the problem. Just when we were getting used to Mick's odd lifestyle in the same evasive way we diminish madness by calling it eccentricity, his story grew darker. Allal moves in with his boyfriend, and the Frenchman is murdered. This was not the sequence but inverting it helps me remove a connection. Though Mick made none either – the killing is remote in all senses of the word – I felt ill at ease, especially as the Frenchman's prophecy had been fulfilled, his garden now, I supposed, an imminent wilderness accommodating the shadows of two men at play. I began to fear for Mick as I never had before. I saw a story-teller about to be engulfed by the events he was witnessing. There followed an appeal for money, and the first hints of friction between Mick and Allal over the state of the garden, the future of the house. With the Frenchman gone, I could imagine anarchy displacing a nominal, exotic order. There is talk of occupying the building. A lawyer's emissary is seen off by Allal and his companion amid much laughter. Others move in. Mick sends a letter of disturbing incoherence. Then a postcard from Algiers. Then nothing. Some of this I share with Molly and the rest, and I suppose that what I don't share is the magnitude of the difference between us. There is little we can do. Little I can do.

Molly and I often stand on the landing as evening closes in, gazing through the stained glass window for Mick's next unannounced homecoming. That dotty architect designed things so that the declining sun, summer and winter, strikes the glass, filling the top of the house with diffused, kaleidoscopic colour. At other times, and these depend on one's momentary feeling or point of view, it is the affect of the glass on our external surroundings – the garden, the road, the meadow, the tree-fringed mountain, the silvered estuary nicked into faraway cliffs – which appeals to us as we hold fast to our anchorage.

Peter, with his metropolitan unconcern and his deepening imperviousness to shock and surprise, tells us not to worry. Jed and Maria, now parents themselves, are absorbed totally with child-rearing and have neither the time nor the desire to ponder the bothersome forms of its end result. (In any case, Jed has been promoted, and it seems to me that if one is involved in betterment and its spiralling elevations, the plight of those who have free-fallen into life cannot inspire by their example or move by their weaknesses and shortcomings.)

It's almost a year now since any of us heard from Mick. Molly and I keep the postcards in an album, slotting them into polythene cases so that we can view the scene and read the message, itself never expressing more than a holiday-maker's transient pleasure. We keep the few airmails tucked away. I don't blame Molly for continuing to remain perplexed, a state in which indignity and anguish keep colliding. Yet, when I re-read the letters and scan the post-cards, particularly the first one of Trafalgar Square, I can't help thinking that each is an affirmation of intent like nothing we will ever know. It searches us out. When we glimpse it, the effect is unnerving, and we step back, secure in our foothold. Ours is one house, one family, one refuge. But it goes on and on in our imagination, enfolding other families, other refuges disturbed by waywardness and pain and other windows looking out on peril and adventure under open skies.

Unfinished Symphony

Billy can hear the sea in the distance. It's not a roar, but something grumbling. It sounds especially wretched because now, an hour after sunset, no one is taking any notice of it, certainly not the rest of them up at the house. Below the marching pines, waves are flaying Breakers' Point against their will and he imagines that the retreating surf is the blood of the headland, seeping into the mist.

The garden – not much more than a lawn with a concrete path at the side and some wind-bent bushes – slopes towards the water after jutting straight out. The man who sold them the house said it would make a fine terrace, though why he hadn't created one in the twenty years he'd been there was a mystery. Perhaps he had no money to pay anyone to do it. He seemed odd – spindly and slightly overbalanced, like his shrubs – and dressed as if to go out to somewhere official. His mind seemed to be elsewhere, certainly not on gardening. Billy notices how the cusp of the lawn, the middle section which bears the brunt of the wind off the sea, is parched. His father said the man was going into a home.

That's perhaps why he was dressed up, Billy thinks. For the journey. There were two other men with him who said a few words to his father and mother before taking away their prisoner. In the empty garage, there's a light patch on the floor where the man's car, a grey Riley Elf, once stood, and in the middle of it a pool of oil still being soaked up by a scattering of sawdust.

Billy reaches the bottom of the lawn, where deep steps take him to a sloping buttress of stones medalled with ochre lichen. In front of him the pines loom. The way ahead looks steep but it isn't: with care, it's possible to descend to the coastal path. There's a stupid gate on to this path with nothing either side of it, so that the garden really extends to the cliff's edge above the Devil's Whirlpool and its boiling water. But Billy knows this from a previous visit with the estate agent.

Now he's more interested in the garden next door. Unlike the one behind him, in front of his new home, it has been planted with palms and other bushes in different shades of green, and this effort to stall the runaway land has made the grass look healthier. Here and there are dark sculptures – some freestanding, others on plinths – which look as if they have been hauled up from the whirlpool, plundered from the Devil. Some have holes in them, others resemble human forms not quite come into being from their stony tombs. An effort has been made to encompass the first twelve feet of falling land in the area of the pines, in this case more densely planted, and it is here, in the half-light, that Billy sees a real human figure start walking away, like something wild revealing its camouflage by the meanest of movement. He gets the impression that he has been watched. He can hear twigs cracking faintly underfoot and what sounds like whistling and singing becoming softer and softer. Then, through a hole in one of the sculptures, a tiny silhouette appears and stops for a few seconds before vanishing over the brow of the land.

'Billy!' his mother shouts. 'Tea's ready. Spencer's here.'

He can see her on the upper horizon where the lawn starts its seaward curve. Everything about her is billowing, like a flag in a gale – her long brown hair, her dress, her woolly cardigan. It's as if she has come not to retrieve him but to form an alliance with him against some enemy not yet visible behind her. Because of this, he rushes up the hill so that she can see that he's heard her summons, at which point she turns and heads back to the house.

For Spencer's benefit, they arrived in time to see the sunset. Spencer was late, but in any case the spectacle fizzled out in a bank of cloud moving up the channel. The anti-climax brought darkness forward by an hour and the lathering sea below the garden grew ominous. Billy doesn't mind admitting fear of the dark, of the shadows, but he wishes it wouldn't change things. Behind him, the waves are wilful and flinging their spume madly.

Spencer Lockwood probably hates him – ever since he came home early from school that afternoon with the sniffles and found Spencer and Meryl playing horse and rider in her bedroom. This was in the other house. Spencer was angry: he stood silently above him, zipping his trousers. 'Don't you dare say anything,' Meryl scolded. There was an odd smell in the room. They were going to get married once Spencer started teaching. Billy thinks he wouldn't fancy being in Spencer Lockwood's class, not after he'd caught him shagging his sister. As the house wobbles closer, he chants under his breath, 'Shagger Lockwood, Shagger Lockwood.' He spots Spencer's car, a sky-blue sports job, parked at a crazy angle, as if about to shoot off any minute towards the Devil's Whirlpool. He imagines the car spinning in the water and Spencer, trouserless, threatening him unavailingly as he sinks deeper, going round and round like a blurred Catherine Wheel.

'And what have you been up to?' Meryl asks. Spencer, his mouth full of chocolate cupcake, smirks at him as he passes. He ignores his sister's inquiry by walking away, so that his own question floats free for anyone to answer: 'Who lives next door?'

His father is standing near the table, taking a stethoscope apart. Already, there's a sign nailed to the gate: Roderick Mahon, MD, BCh. Billy has never heard anyone except his mother call him Roderick, only Roddy – Dr Roddy Mahon. His mother calls him Roderick when she's uptight and impatient, which has been pretty often of late.

'Her name is Alice Westerway,' his father says. 'She's a composer.' He supplies the information indifferently, as though already the woman has entered his circle and, in due course, will be introduced to the new doctor's twelve-year-old son.

'I've seen her,' Billy says. 'She's creepy. What do you mean, a composer?'

'What do you think he means?' Spencer asks.

They are all like this, never telling him anything, always expecting him to give an answer so that he can prove that either he's not stupid or they're superior or both.

'She writes music,' his mother says, passing by on one of

her motherly tasks. He senses that she doesn't like these games the others play with him. She brings them to a close before they can get properly started.

By 'music' his mother probably means the gramophone records his father plays in the evenings. Mostly it sounds gloomy – when it's not rattling the walls. He has seen his mother go up to the hi-fi without being asked and turn the volume down. His father never complains about this: it's as if he has simply forgotten to do it himself, though he never says 'Thank you'. Spencer likes traditional jazz. When he talks about it, his father remains silent, nodding as spittle slides down his pipe stem. 'Trad' jazz is always muffled, and comes from Meryl's bedroom when Spencer is visiting.

A few days later, Dr Mahon calls Billy to the living room. On the radio is a piece of music by Alice Westerway called 'Ocean Murmurs'. As Billy listens, his father stares at him, looking puzzled, before starting to make a repeated figure eight with his right palm. It sounds to Billy like the music he hears at the cinema, except now there's no-one in the clinches, no galleon with Gregory Peck aboard, no pictures whatever, except his father towering over him in a trance. When the music ends, ghostly people begin to clap.

'I expect she wrote it after listening to the sea down below,' his father says. Billy is expected to accept this opinion as the last word. His father picks up *The Cornishman* and hides behind it, as he always does when there's no more to be said – about anything. Smoke signals rise above the newspaper.

Billy's bedroom window overlooks Alice Westerway's garden. For hours, he never sees her, though lights go on in the house at night. She has an old car that sinks down at the back: Spencer says the springs have gone. When she starts the engine, it farts clouds of grey smoke. She never goes out after dark. He wonders whether she will become one of his father's patients.

'Your father cannot go collecting people like butterflies,' his mother explains when he asks. 'But if she wants to be on daddy's list, I expect he will accept her.' He has heard them talking about patients after surgery or after his father has had to rush out late at night following a phone call. His mother does most of it while his father rests his head in his hands. He thinks of his grandmother at these times, how she used to ask him if he'd lost his tongue. She must have said it a lot to his father as well, when he was a boy.

He is thinking of this when Meryl announces that she and Spencer are getting married. He feels this should be a happy moment but Spencer stands in the background fidgeting and looking serious. Later, from his room upstairs, Billy can hear his father's raised voice as an argument starts below. His mother runs up the stairs and slams a door behind her. Tip-toeing towards it, he can hear her sobbing. Then, from the landing, he sees his father rushing to the front door. As he fumbles with the knob and eventually pulls the door open, Alice Westerway is standing there. She is small, like a jenny wren, and her bony hands are clasped in front of her chest.

'I did knock,' Billy hears her say. 'But...'

'That's all right,' his father says. 'What can I do for you?'

Billy doesn't hear the next bit but his mother, now standing behind him, does and trots down the stairs. They escort Alice Westerway into the front room, leaving Meryl and Spencer in the hall to wonder what's up.

It turns out that Alice Westerway has chest pains. Billy's

father told her not to worry, it was probably indigestion, a spot of acid in the tummy. But her visit has had a calming affect. Afterwards, he sees his mother, his father, his sister and Spencer sitting around the dining-room table, talking. They look like four people in a restaurant, waiting to be served. From his bedroom widow, he can see Alice Westerway's house in darkness. He tries to stare through the gloom. And within seconds, the lights come on, almost as if he had willed it. Spencer and Meryl walk arm in arm to the car. As it moves off, the back wheels spin on the gravel, sending a hail of stones into the shrubbery.

The next morning, a Saturday, Billy's mother asks him if he would like Alice Westerway to teach him to play the piano. His father is smoking his pipe in the corner, his face turned towards them to catch the reply.

'But we haven't got a piano,' Billy says.

'We'll buy one,' his father explains. 'That's not a problem.'

It's always like this: his mother asking the questions, trying to draw things out of him, while his father stands aside, blocking his exits.

'OK,' Billy says, and as he does so his father slides a record out of its sleeve, taking care to hold it only in the middle, and places it two-handed on the turntable. His father sits and watches him as the LP – piano music – is playing. He won't say anything. Billy sometimes imagines Spencer and his father having a battle with their gramophones, firing jazz and classical music at each other, except that neither would give in, both would retreat and play their music to themselves.

Billy spends Sunday morning thinking about his mother's offer. But the weather is so good that it slips his mind as he plays in the garden. Meryl and Spencer are spending the weekend at Spencer's parents' home in Plymouth. Mr and Mrs Lockwood came for a meal one day, at the other house. Mr Lockwood wore a cap, which he rolled up and stuffed in his jacket pocket. Arms outstretched, Billy is dive-bombing Nazis on the ridge where the garden begins its descent. As he banks to the right, he spies his mother at the front upstairs window. She is looking for her paints. 'Be careful,' she shouts, above his father's music.

After lunch, Dr Roddy Mahon clicks shut his black box of tricks and walks down the lane towards Alice Westerway's house. It's built of grey stone and slate tiles, and the terracotta chimney stack wears a coronet of splashed seagull shit. It seems to Billy that the house is carved from rock that has always been there, whereas their own house, their new house, perched higher at the end of the lane and with its brown pebble-dash, bow windows and thick ornamental tiled roof, is out of place. Alice Westerway's house invites the wind and the rain and the sea's quiet murmur, while their own sends it away to pester some other place, Mr and Mrs Lockwood's perhaps. Spencer told Billy that as a boy he would climb into the loft of his house and walk fifty yards in opposite directions above the bedroom ceilings of the neighbours, all twenty-five of them, including a Mr Bamford, who lived on his own and later put his head in the oven. Billy's father has already been into the loft of their new house with a torch. 'Come on up and have a look, Billy,' he shouted through the black trap door in a voice like God's.

It is his mother who breaks the news brought back by his father.

'I'm sorry, Billy,' she says, bending on one knee and

adjusting his shirt collar even though it needs no attention. 'Mrs Westerway doesn't give lessons, only to older pupils.'

He's noticed how grown-ups say one thing and then say the opposite straight after.

'How old?' he asks.

His father listens to what his mother has to say but has begun cutting old burnt tobacco from inside the bowl of his pipe. It drops into his free hand like apple peel. If he didn't have to do it he would be able to answer Billy's questions himself. But for some reason he is angry. He refers to their neighbour as 'that Westerway woman'.

'Much older,' his mother explains. 'Much older and much cleverer. She is also very busy.'

After this, he regards Alice Westerway, despite her frailty, as someone who has spurned him. He feels sorry for his father, who has had to bring the bad news and hand it to his mother. The other news he brings is that Alice Westerway is taking Milk of Magnesia and has become one of his father's butterflies. Billy hopes she does not start knocking at their door every whipstitch as Mrs Berryman did at their other house. Mrs Berryman needed the doctor once a fortnight but there was nothing wrong with her, unlike his Uncle Trevor, who had everything wrong with him but refused to see one and died. Sometimes, these things make his head buzz.

Now that Spencer is not there to see it – he is probably with Meryl, placing his hand gently on her stomach, because babies at this stage are just tadpoles – the sun begins its dazzling fall into the sea. It will soon be time for dinner. Mr and Mrs Lockwood will have had their dinner six hours earlier and washed up the tea things, and will be listening to hymns on the radio, Mrs Lockwood singing along quietly so as not to disturb her husband. Billy's mother has found her watercolours in one of the packing-cases and is in the top window, painting the sunset and the gold glitter it has cast on the water. Downstairs, his father's face is screwed up with the pain of listening to more music. From Alice Westerway's open French windows comes the piano sounds he will never be taught.

And he wonders how long the Devil has been down there behind him, stirring up trouble in the green waters as the ocean moans its disapproval.

A Point of Dishonour

I knew Islington but I wouldn't say I knew London. My daughter had once lived there, a London 'villager' in that use of the term I always found amusing. Michael Kramer lived in Alwynne Square. It looked almost deserted, except for the odd taxi. City noises were beyond it, in the background. The doors were painted glossy black and the redundant brass door-knockers shone. I'd made an appointment and I was on time. I rang the doorbell.

I could hear no ringing tone inside but a woman answered anyway, opening the door just enough for her to poke her head around it and for me to see that she was wearing some kind of kaftan. Her hair was long, grey and unkempt. She said nothing but raised her eyebrows, obviously inviting me to state my business. Almost immediately, she opened the door wider in response to something said by a man coming down the stairs behind her. He took over as she vanished into the wings. It was Kramer. I remembered him from the photo on the book's dust jacket. He invited me in. There was a copy of the book on the telephone table, and I wondered if he'd placed it there deliberately.

Kramer's book, *A Point of Dishonour*, was about my great-grandfather, Jack Cowperthwaite, or rather, my great-grandfather was one of a number of people featured in it. They had all been court-martialled and shot in the Great War; in most cases for deserting the battlefield. The book's subtitle was, *Men Who Fell Too Early*. It was difficult to tell what Kramer felt about my great-grandfather and his compatriots-in-arms. In one sense he seemed intent on vindicating the military, faced with few if any options when confronted by soldiers who refused to engage in combat; in another, he thought history was not best served by consigning to oblivion those men who may have been psychologically scarred by the bloody scenes they'd witnessed. My great-grandfather Jack, for example, had walked away from the noise and anger of battle in 1918 at Havrincourt, a successful Allied engagement in which three divisions of Sir Julian Byng's Third Army captured the French village against numerically superior forces. In the book, Kramer notes, 'By this late stage in the war the fighting will of the Germans was in decline.' I knew the sections referring to Jack almost by heart. I couldn't believe that most of these 'cowards' had done anything other than given a good account of themselves from the time they'd enlisted to the moment of their lapse. Just being there and going through it must have been a sort of heroism.

I'd been recollecting all this, rehearsing it, before I arrived. Kramer led me up two flights of stairs. I'd exchanged pleasantries with him down below and had noticed the grey-haired woman fussing about and muttering to herself in the kitchen. Before entering his apartment and presumably because we were out of earshot, he explained that the woman was formerly his wife and that they had agreed after their divorce to live separate lives under the same roof. I don't know why he should have told me that. I couldn't help thinking that the ex-wife had been unfairly landed with the job of answering the door.

The apartment was not the kind of bohemian redoubt I might have expected. There was a laptop computer on a table near the back window, and pictures on the wall: some modern, some traditional in gilt frames. Files and books in tidy rows seemed to reflect an orderly mind. A notepad lay open next to the laptop with a fountain pen resting snugly in its hinge. In one corner was a sort of kitchenette. The room was suffused with bright morning light. Kramer invited me to sit in a leather settee, which seemed to engulf me. I felt too much at home too early on.

Standing before me in front of an unused fireplace, Kramer began talking about *A Point Of Dishonour* before I'd had a chance to tell him the reason for my visit. I'd explained in a letter and then in a phone call that I had important information about my great-grandfather and that as I was in London for another reason on that particular day (not true), he might be interested in seeing me.

'You'll have gathered that I don't go into much auto-biographical detail about the unfortunates in the book,' he said, obviously not aware or not worrying that the word 'unfortunates' to my mind further diminished them as individuals.

'I read a review in the Sunday papers, though it didn't mention my great-grandfather or his particular story,' I said.

'So I bought the book, only half-expecting him to be mentioned.'

Leaning forward and smiling, he said: 'It's very expensive!'

Had he summed me up as someone who could ill-afford to part with twenty-five pounds or was he inviting me to deplore the audacity of publishers in charging so much? I couldn't tell. His surroundings obviously suggested that he was more than well-off. He asked me if I would like coffee. I said yes and he went into the kitchenette to brew up.

'So what did you think?' he shouted, clinking cups and saucers.

'You discovered something I never knew,' I said, raising my voice and half-turning towards him to maintain a sort of formality.

'Really? Milk and sugar?'

He returned with the coffee and some biscuits and sat beside me on the settee, leaning towards me with one arm resting lazily across the back of it.

'The incident at Havrincourt. I never knew the details but you don't actually say... you don't express a view about what Jack and the others did.'

'You mean a moral view?'

He looked serious, as though wishing me to tell him precisely why I was there. I didn't want to go into the ethics of war, but I blurted out something: 'Despite what you say about the mental state of Jack and the others, I wondered if you nonetheless believed in honour and disapproved of cowardice.'

He smiled again and raised his eyebrows. I felt stupid. How could anyone approve of cowardice. I wanted to say 'abhorred', but I hadn't thought of the word quickly enough.

'Men,' he said. 'Such uncomplicated beings!'

It sounded like the old defence mechanism: an invitation to accept, and by implication pity, the male for his lack of deviousness.

It was then that I became aware of a distant commotion in the house: raised voices, which I took to be a heated phone call, then doors slamming and the clatter of pots and pans. Kramer talked over them without explanation, though he must have seen that I was alarmed. Even when the front door shut with such a bang that the apartment's front window rattled, he merely fell silent for a few seconds, sighed heavily, and carried on.

The coffee drained, I felt he wanted me to press ahead. Jack and his story had taken up a whole page in the book. He didn't ask what my information was and I needed a context to introduce it. I told him a bit about myself, my interests.

'I'm keen on family history,' I said, trying not to lead up to the dramatic act I wished to avoid. 'It's a bit boring really. Jack was an only child of parents with siblings who had died in infancy. Tracing the family on his side has been difficult. I've begun researching more fruitful branches of the family tree. However, I've retained an interest in Jack for obvious reasons.'

I told him more about my family on both sides. I'm sure he did find this boring. Like all family-historians, I supplied too much detail. He continued to smile at me as a parent does when indulging a child in its elaborate fantasies. At one stage, affecting to make himself more comfortable, he discreetly slid towards me, crossing his legs.

I reminded Kramer that Jack was 28 when he was

executed. 'At that age, I had begun moving up the career ladder at Kendal, Milne and Faulkner's, the Manchester department store.'

'I know it,' he said quickly. Something told me that he didn't. He said he'd gone to Leeds Grammar School and then Oxford University to study history, but I knew that from the book's dust jacket. He added: 'And now?'

'Head buyer.'

He looked impressed. I wanted to say that we were alike, similarly 'privileged': at our feet the same world, one not without conflict somewhere but holding out more promise than disappointment. But I thought it might encourage him in his attempts to ingratiate himself with me, his wish to slide further along the settee. He spoke as though Jack had been his relative too. Then we began to talk about what had happened to Jack on the Western Front.

I knew the story by heart. My great-grandfather had been involved in an attack on the northern flank in three successive waves, right to left, and directly west towards the village. The first wave made ground under light machine-gun fire, encouraging the second to follow quickly. But by the time this middle wave had reached halfway along its route, the machine-gunners had been reinforced on both sides (possibly, Kramer believes, by two positions, or 'nests', caught unawares by the first charge) and several of the advancing soldiers were felled by a sweep of gunfire along the whole flank. Jack was in the third wave. For some reason the subaltern commanding decided that this final charge should take on the machine-gun post immediately opposite, leaving the soldiers exposed to angled crossfire from the other two. Whatever the option, this wave, like the second, came under heavy fire from all three posts. Jack must have seen a dozen of his colleagues killed before he halted, turned and walked back to his own line. At the court martial, it was said that the cowardice of his withdrawal had been 'somewhat mitigated' by his decision to retreat by walking rather than running, the suggestion presumably being that he had increased his chances of dying with his colleagues, despite the 'quintessential shame' (Kramer's phrase) of being shot in the back. However, the court also heard that the Germans had ceased firing when they saw Jack walking away. Kramer says this was probably a lie which no-one was fussed to contest. He makes much of the 'lie' on the page dealing with Jack, and it crops up elsewhere in the book. If the lie could be established as such, he says, Jack's action could be construed as a kind of bravery or, at the very least, a calamitous disregard for his own safety.

After a while, I had told him everything, save one story, the reason for my visit. I was about to reach in my handbag for the cutting from the *Westmorland Gazette* when the front door slammed shut again. A woman's voice shouted 'Michael!' with an interrogative snarl. Kramer waved his hand in front of him to minimise any concern I might have, rose from the settee and went downstairs, closing the apartment door behind him.

In the muffled exchange below, the woman's voice was raised and agitated, Kramer's quiet and pacifying. All went still and he returned to the apartment and the settee, by which time I had retrieved the cutting and was reading it. I think he said 'Where were we?' but I may have imagined that. I handed him the cutting; it was thin and browned with age, but its type was still readable after ninety-nine years; it seemed to hold a secret always available, like an imperishable indictment. Above the text was a short ladder of headlines in letters of descending size. At the top it read 'Penrith Man Rained Blows On Young Wife', then 'Child Saw Fracas', followed by 'Showed No Remorse'. It told how my great-grandfather, aged twenty, had come home drunk and beaten his wife unconscious in front of their four-year-old daughter. The report was largely given over to the comments of the presiding magistrate, though the bench heard how Jack Cowperthwaite had had a history of violence in his neighbourhood, on one occasion towards a girl he had been courting before his marriage to Mary Jane Cowperthwaite (née Howgill). In his defence, it was stated that my great-grandfather, a labourer on his wife's parents' farm, was noted for consuming 'alcoholic liquor' in huge quantities, though he had tried to give up drink with the help of the Society of Rechabites in Carlisle. Jack Cowperthwaite spent two years in Lancaster Jail. The undeclared remorse was something noted by a policeman at the scene.

Kramer looked at me, also a Howgill, shrugged his shoulders and handed back the cutting. He obviously hadn't known about its contents. Not that they were of use to him. He became curt, as if I had deliberately tried to embarrass him, and he twice looked at his watch without saying anything about soon having to attend to something else. There was no other way of introducing Jack's background story, no soft-bedded context. But in a way, I wanted it to be dramatic. Seeking a way of doing that without having him dismiss the information before sliding further towards me had proved impossible. Perhaps I'm over-sensitive. Perhaps Michael Kramer, in old Westmoreland dialect, was 'a man o' harns', a brainy type, whose interest in what I'd come to say was only academic.

'Well, that's it,' he said. 'I don't know what else there is. It's all in the book.'

He made it sound as though I'd disappointed him. I suppose I had, although in what sense I wasn't sure. I shouldn't have gone there. I don't know what made me. But something did. Something that still nags me about what we think of people and what we know of them.

He pointed to the cutting folded in my hand: 'Let me copy that. It might come in useful if there's a second edition of the book.'

I gave him the report again. He went over to a machine in the corner, sandwiched the cutting and buzzed a copy. He held it up as if he were performing a magician's trick for a country dweller, a woman furthermore, who might not know what a printer was.

Our meeting was over. He asked if I would like him to mail me a signed copy of the book rather than get me to send him mine for that purpose. I said yes and gave him my address. For some odd reason I wanted to tell him that Jack returned to the farm on his release from prison in the summer of 1912 to find the men of the Howgill and Cowperthwaite families ranged against him, arms folded. It was part of the complete story. But I forgot. Suddenly it seemed to be irrelevant and uninteresting, like the branches of my tortuous family tree. Before I left and despite his change of mood, Kramer asked me where I was staying and whether I'd like to join him for dinner that evening at a West End restaurant. 'I can book a table for two,' he said. So not there, at home, with his strange wife. I said I was visiting friends and staying with them overnight. I declined his invitation. He said it had been an interesting meeting and shut the front door quietly behind me. Looking back, I saw his wife's face at one of the lower windows.

Later the next day, having fled London and stayed overnight at a motorway hotel, I was driving across the fell, past weatherbeaten holdings where the ghosts of those menacing sentinels could still be imagined barring entrance. I have long been familiar with the countryside between the M6 and the Pennines, which come into view at all high points beyond Orton on roads west: Great Asby Scar and its limestone pavements, for example. The terrain here is as bleak as it must have been centuries ago when the farms of Drybeck, huddled beneath it, first bedded down for winter. This is not land in which hedgerows have been torn out to create bigger, more manageable fields in the name of progress and to meet demand. Anyone can sense that patterns of life here, as well as the arrangements and ownership of pasture, have remained mostly unchanged, the world merely having brought small improvements in ways of dealing with them. Not even the names vary that much. My husband's a different Howgill from the family of my cowering great-grandmother, but no doubt somewhere along the line they were connected, if only in the sense of being survivors in the same harsh, unforgiving region.

A year has gone by and I'm still waiting for the signed copy of Kramer's book. In the circumstances, perhaps I was a bit hard on him.

In The Beginning

It was the least he could do, his daughter told him. Stuck up there in his eyrie, looking down on the rest of the world – and spying.

From his window on the top floor of the RapidTrans building, he looks directly across at Korda into the room provided rent-free at Jill's prompting. He and Korda have never met but he believes it may soon be time for the end of his snooping. Making the room available to Korda isn't much of a gesture in monetary terms, which is just as well, because Ferenc Korda has no collateral, apparently not even a change of clothes. Each day, the wizened Hungarian appears in the window with his bundle of mail, chuckles to himself and begins opening the envelopes with a blade that occasionally flashes like distant semaphore.

Perhaps he's giggling at the name of his benefactor, the man staring at him unbeknown across the way – Sam Johnson, head of the country's fastest-growing haulage company – or at the coincidence of Johnson's physical elevation in the building with the recent move of RapidTrans into air freight. Sometimes, old Korda is joined by a young female assistant, who wears her spectacles at the end of her nose and sits cross-legged with a notebook, like a stenographer in an old Hollywood film. While 'spying', Johnson stands back from the window so that he can't be seen.

The RapidTrans building is shaped like a closed staple, so that the gap between them is no more than thirty feet. Yet they take circuitous and opposite routes to their stations and have never acknowledged each other, at least not informally, even across their wind-blown divide, where seagulls often skew wildly upwards, their reflections distorted in the high windows. Korda sent him a brief letter of thanks for the room, typed with a jumping letter 'o' on the back of a torn-off advert for odourless garlic capsules. The room is at the end of a slightly larger area containing the company's employee records – those who have retired after long service and those still ploughing the furrow – intended for Johnson's stalled adventure in company history and nostalgia. Part of his reason for looking across at Korda is to envision the scheme as up and running, with Korda the man in charge of maintaining contact with former RapidTrans staff and producing a thrice-yearly newsletter. The Hungarian's grubby black suit seems appropriate for someone who would be recording deaths and achievements as much as pursuing the activities of the elderly.

But Korda's zeal is emptied into running an obscure poetry magazine called *Genesis*. Jill came across it while researching her doctorate on the tradition of small literary publications. Small, she assured her father, referred to circulation rather than influence. 'You mean like muggers,' he said provocatively. Korda is anything but an opportunist and, as a man possibly in his early seventies, could well have come to Britain as a young adult after the Soviet invasion. A victim, therefore. He is almost comic, with tufts of grey hair spiralling outwards from behind his ears. Anyway, Jill convinced her father that old Korda, awash with manuscripts and memorabilia in a Peckham basement flat, needed a system and space to survive. Johnson's suggestion was typically bold, reckless even.

Johnson himself will soon be eligible for inclusion in his imagined newsletter, not as a footnote beneath a passport photograph but as someone meriting an edition of his own: the single-minded founder of RapidTrans, already gliding from his summit towards the region of slow dancers and faltering music, where only one outcome is certain. It's a prospect that has turned a chummy nature into one which is almost inconversable. He has become morose for the first time in his life. He is a figurehead, but his minions now take him for granted.

Korda never looks across directly; if he appears close to the window at all it is to gaze down at the ornamental lake – once part of the docks – while dictating something to his secretary. She holds her notebook in front of her face and scribbles away almost as if she were pretending unsuccessfully to be something she is not. Her hair is bound in the shape of candyfloss on a stick, which Johnson vaguely remembers as a 'beehive' style. Once, it began to come adrift: a kiss-curl dropped on to her forehead as she was taking notes. When she is not there, Korda spends hours licking buff envelopes, and often rests his head on clenched fists, as though observing some sort of religious rite or journeying in the depths of memory.

One of the conditions of tenancy, apart from Korda's understanding that he is to offer no money for the magazine's lodging, is isolation. Johnson told his daughter to explain that the office should be viewed as a public footpath across private land: in effect, Korda owned it and was simply establishing his rights. After the message was delivered, Johnson thought it might have sounded patronising, but Korda said nothing. So far, no-one had questioned Korda's coming and going, though Johnson decreed that it should be no secret: if questions are asked, let them be answered, he told his senior managers. He has since heard the tenancy referred to as 'Sam's whimsy'. Anyway, no-one ventures to Korda's room or even to the records department of which it is an extension, because they have no need to. Johnson sometimes muses on Korda's panting progress to the tenth floor (the lift in that part of the 'staple' goes only to the eighth) and his passage through all those records of lives spent working, which hang suspended in their folders on metal rails. He's been reading up on poetry since Korda moved in. A poem, he has learned, is a song to forgotten lives. The last time he read a poem was as a schoolboy and even then under sufferance. He is tying to recall its details when the office messenger knocks at the door and enters with his mail. Among it is an envelope of the sort that Korda is forever licking and addressing. It bears a white stick-on label with Johnson's name scribbled across it. Inside is the current edition of *Genesis*. The cover is glossy, professionally produced and consists of a photograph of a boxer wearing what looks like a Lonsdale belt, with the name of the magazine and a description of its contents overprinted.

Apart from a photo credit to one Manfred Bauer on the inside front cover, there appears to be no further reference to the boxer or boxing. There are many poems interspersed among pages of densely printed prose, and he notices that a word at the end of one stanza has been Tippexed out and over-typed in a different font. For the moment, he does not examine *Genesis* closely but catches the whiff of a region from which he is excluded. The names of its contributors mean nothing to him, but at the end of a one-page editorial bewailing the costs of printing and urging subscribers to remain loyal and recruit a friend is stamped F. KORDA, EDITOR. Jill has told him that *Genesis* was founded in 1958, a fact confirmed in parenthesis on page two. He peers into the envelope. There is no covering letter, not even one written on the remaining half of an advertisement for homeopathic garlic.

For some time, there has been no need for Sam Johnson to turn up at RapidTrans every day. Amusingly for a company that moves freight, it runs itself. The assumption of his dispensable status simply coincided with his interest in Ferenc Korda and the magazine, so that he now buys his lunch down in the re-modelled docklands (it's full of baguette shops and wine bars) and sits back from his window, watching the slow motion of the enterprise to which he has thrown some sort of lifeline. Korda keeps irregular hours. Some days he makes no appearance; on others he is there first thing and leaves late. He, too, eats sandwiches and drinks from a Thermos flask, which early in the morning of a few cold days steamed like a factory chimney. Korda wipes his mouth with the sleeve of his jacket. In the middle of the afternoon he eats an apple or a banana. Once inside the room, he never leaves the building until it is time to go home.

Johnson has noticed that when Korda stands well back from the window and his door into the records room is closed, he cannot properly be seen. So, two days ago, Johnson bought a pair of miniature binoculars; the green sort easily tucked away in a birdwatcher's rattle-bag. Sitting upstage, as it were, from his own window, he has been training it on Korda. There is the thinnest of stripes in the Hungarian's suit and on his right forefinger a large gold ring mounted with an emerald. In close-up Korda can be seen reading aloud from manuscripts when the secretary is not there, presumably for the pleasure of doing so or to discover if a poem improves by being vocalised. He can see it is a poem by its shape on the page but he cannot decipher the words. For some strange reason he thinks Korda might speak with an accent which has lost everything bar some tell-tale rolled Rs. It is a long time since Johnson, among foreigners, drove lorries at steady speeds across the Low Countries and on the Autobahns, with that picture of Mary and the boys clipped to the windscreen alongside a separate one of Jill on her own. There was always the hint of a forced smile on Mary's face at that time, the smile of someone stoically suppressing pain; but she hadn't let on until it was too late. Korda, he now notices, wears a hearing-aid and has a faint tic, a twitch in the face muscles as though they were recalling something with a tendency to drift. The comparison makes him uneasy. He is reminded of that print of a Francis Bacon picture which some gauche interior designer thought fit for the boardroom. He had it removed.

In Johnson's OUT tray lies the draft of the financial report for the shareholders' meeting. RapidTrans is freewheeling.

Always an advocate of delegation, he sometimes wishes a reverse of the process so that he could claim more than a founding credit for the company's success. He picks up his copy of *Genesis* and suddenly recalls that schoolboy poem. It was Tennyson's *Morte D'Arthur*. He begins mouthing the lines, and amusingly they seem to be relevant as he watches Korda, perched at the summit of the building like a nonchalant mountaineer:

> The bare black cliff clang'd round him, as he based
> His feet on juts of slippery crag that rang
> Sharp-smitten with the dint of armed heels –

He puts the magazine down and lifts the binoculars again. Suddenly, Korda is standing at the window with his hands behind his back and this time looking his way. But there is no contact. Korda turns and leaves the room, an old man taken short.

The route follows the staple's shape: down in the lift, along a corridor, a ninety-degree turn, a slightly longer stretch, another turn, a lengthy haul past Reception, another right-angle, a further corridor and turn, then the lift to the eighth floor. Johnson takes the two short flights of stairs quietly. At the foot of the second, he can hear a cistern re-filling. As he walks down the middle of the Records room towards Korda's open door, he notices that the files are moving on their hooks, buffeted by someone who has recently passed by or sucked into the slipstream.

The journey through the edifice of RapidTrans, his memorial made concrete, leaves Johnson dizzy. Perhaps it really is time for him to go. He remembers a few more lines of that Tennyson poem. He repeats them silently to himself, though his lips move, approaching some memorable region of speech. Korda is sitting hunched over the desk with his back to him, the hillocked back of a burden-carrier, and only when Johnson is looking down does Korda turn and ripple for a second with fright.

'Ferenc Korda?' Johnson inquires, his voice rising to the final syllable.

Hotel De La Paix

Tiny Mr Kesselman is in the garden again, fussing over his buttonhole and looking back at the building as though he owns it. From where Bobby Samson sits in one of the attic windows, staring down at him, he really does seem small, but it's his comic self-importance rather than his size or his pride in appearance that makes everyone smile. Beyond the garden, the formal part that leads the eye down to the lake, clouds are leaving the mountains to hover as mist above the water, offering a glimpse of snow-capped peaks.

'I know autumn is here because we need the light on,' says Greta, who is stretched out on the divan with her hands behind her head.

'Don't put it on yet,' Bobby says, without looking away. 'Old Kesselman might think I'm spying.'

'Mr Kesselman is in a world of his own. He'll probably believe you're sympathising with him. You're the sympathetic sort.'

They have all succumbed to the stability of the lake. Even in squally weather the revisions on its normally glacial surface seem like affronts, and they respond accordingly, becoming irritated while waiting for its restoration. They have arrived in Switzerland seeking not so much peace after the tumults of war but the continuity of peace, proof that somewhere beyond the battle lines it has always existed undisturbed. Of course, there are issues concerning neutrality in a place where the expatriates talk a lot about politics and reconstruction, even to the extent of wondering if neutrality in the circumstances of the recent past belonged to the category of craven acts. But they have come to embrace the land, not so much its people. And the lake, deep, windless and smooth-surfaced, mirrors their long-held need for rest and tranquility.

Bobby, Greta, Mr Kesselmann and the others occupy rooms in the hotel's converted attic space. It's a big, famous hotel so the space is huge, and chilly when it's cold outside. However, they work long hours and are happy to do so, the better it seems to make the new lives they desire for themselves.

In a few minutes, Bobby has to put on his waiter's uniform and take the lift to the dining-room. There he will linger near the door for two hours while the guests have tea. Lingering – being unobtrusive but always on hand – is one of the arts he has learned since arriving a month ago in his 'civvy' suit and with his dyed RAF greatcoat over his arm. He has also learned that Mr Kesselman, though having fled persecution, has not arrived in a country entirely free of prejudice. Greta says one overhears much when rendering oneself invisible, in some circumstances the only bonus of servitude. Greta is a housemaid and a psychologist-in-waiting.

Bobby and Greta are good friends and see each other often. He believes they both sense some unspoken knowledge about each other. Still, they have spent a lot of time together in the past few weeks. He finds this odd, but he guesses she behaves in exactly the same way with other men when she is not in his company; in fact, he saw her laughing and flicking her hair back in a way he recognised when he passed the Café Vendome on his bicycle the other day. One of his colleagues, Lorenz, and a woman he didn't recognise were sitting at the table with her, drinking coffee. The town has been full of such people since the war ended – young, carefree individuals mellowed by events or reports of them. They are a community, whose members are still getting to know each other. Mr Kesselman is excluded from it for at least three reasons: he is older, he keeps to himself and the origins of his arrival lay not in the war itself but in pre-war intimations of trouble, which the end of the conflict has vindicated in the most ghastly fashion. He has told Greta as much, partly because of anxiety about scattered relatives. Bobby is aware that Greta's friendships are of equal intensity, whether they be with men or women. If anything, the little group of females to which she is attached exudes a collusive air. Some of the local men – expatriates sarcastically call them 'the observer corps' – have a reputation for leering. Bobby's breath is condensing on the window pane, and through the opaque cloud a fly leaves tracks like footprints in snow.

Greta often comes to his room to spend an hour or so with him. They share the same taste in books and the merger of their vague ideas on some subjects results in a clarification of view. In a way, they enjoy an intimacy that has no need of consummation, though they often touch each other affectionately, like a couple who have already enjoyed carnal pleasure and found it wanting. He leaves Mr Kesselman to his fantasies and approaches the dressing-table, where Greta is waiting for him to brush her hair. They chat, watching their conversation reported back to them.

'Who's on with you today?' she asks.

'Lorenz,' he says. 'Do you know what his name means?'

'No.'

'Laurel. A bit tame, don't you think – to be named after a bush, and a poisonous one at that?'

'You British are so dim. Do you not see him wreathed in leaves, like a victorious warrior?'

He tugs at her hair so that she winces. She is forever making statements that bear unintentionally on his immediate past, when he flew sorties over Germany and looked down fixedly on a rectangle of moonlit landscape hurtling like a newsreel out of control. Mostly when some indiscretion flies from her lips she straightaway raises her hand in apology. He just stares at her, waiting for the pictures she has summoned to vanish.

'I saw you together at the café,' he says. 'You seemed to be hitting it off.'

'There you go,' she says. 'Together. You couldn't possibly mean sitting at the same table having an intelligent conversation. You mean bonded, two of a kind, all of a piece.'

'How do you know what I mean?'

'Are you jealous, Bobby?'

'What – of you?'

She looks up at him in the mirror, wondering if she should suggest that Lorenz, not she, is the object of his affection.

She knows that so soon after a time when every move made by Bobby and his colleagues led to destruction, no decision about anything major is taken lightly. So often, when not working, they meditate alone beside the brooding lake. You could see them – Bobby, Greta, Lorenz, Mr Kesselmann – treading the shoreline's naked shingles.

The waiters take it in turns to preside at tea-time in pairs, standing opposite each other at the circular room's two entrances. It is not their function to interrupt the buffet-style ceremony, in which sandwiches and pieces of cake are taken from salvers, and tea and coffee are poured from urns, but they replenish the table and relieve guests of their empty cups and plates. The clientele, mainly older Americans and Northern Europeans with money, are not voracious feeders, preferring to take what they need at one go rather than have a healthy appetite interpreted as bad manners. Lorenz, approaching him as they were sweeping up crumbs, once likened the thin widows among them to sparrows. The duty waiters are not so far removed from each other that they cannot smile across the room at an observation confirmed. Lorenz's smile is broad and generous and accompanied by a chuckle as his chest beneath the starched shirt imperceptibly shakes.

Lorenz is about Bobby's age and comes from a village a few miles from Versoix. It amuses Bobby to compare him to the idealised Germans he once shot out of the skies: blond, suntanned, unmarked, and with a lofty superiority related more to bearing than height. For the same reasons, Mr Kesselman, the oldest waiter among them but in other respects their equal, seems to find the comparison unsettling: at any rate, Lorenz is the one with whom Mr

Kesselman has the least contact, not avoiding him exactly but also not going out of his way to be friendly. Greta says Mr Kesselman needs to take care, or else the turmoil fomented inside him by Lorenz's presence could lead to trouble. The psychologist in her says character is often ascribed to a person's origins rather than to a capacity for sullenness.

'I like Lorenz,' Greta says. 'He's a mystery.'

'What do you mean, a mystery?'

'He's inscrutable. You just don't know where you are with him. I find that interesting.'

'You would – you're a psychologist.'

She shudders again. They have all declared themselves to each other, but only Bobby tosses their avowals back at them when it suits him. Bobby is not prepared to jostle freely, to leave himself exposed in the open.

'Then let me practise on you.'

She stands up, snatching the brush, and wrestles him towards the bed. He collapses on to it, laughing. While he lies there waiting for her interrogation to begin, she draws up a chair, grabs a book and pencil and pretends to take notes. He hears the insect-like abrasion of her stockings as she crosses her legs.

'Now, Mr Samson. What did you do in the war?'

'I was a bomb-aimer.'

'What did this involve?'

'Being regularly frightened out of my wits.'

'Why do you want to be a waiter in Switzerland?'

'It seemed like a good idea at the time.'

'What are your intentions towards me?'

'Platonic.' He grins.

'Thanks very much. Did you lose friends in the war?'

'Yes.'

'What was your greatest fear?'

'Having to ditch in the sea.'

'Can you swim?'

'No.'

'Would you like me to teach you?'

'Maybe.'

'Can I put the light on now?'

'Yes.'

Before flicking the switch, she goes to the window as if in response to Bobby's reservations about Mr Kesselman. But Mr Kesselman is nowhere to be seen. The guests are on the lawn, enjoying cigarettes before tea. They have their backs to her. Some of them are staring out towards the lake, as if having witnessed some strange watery happening now subdued and disappeared from sight. Their personal plumes of smoke give the impression that they are on fire and don't yet know it. She feels privy to impending disaster, like a clairvoyant.

'What are your intentions towards Lorenz?' she asks suddenly, without turning around to face him. He reaches up and puts on the light himself. Her face is immediately reflected back at him in the window, as though a stranger looking into the room from outside has joined them and is also seeking an answer to her question.

'What do you mean?'

'The mystery of Lorenz is that he tries to reach other people through a third party, namely me.'

'And?'

'I think he'd like to get to know you.' She suddenly feels

that, for a moment, meditation is over and decision-making has begun. Bobby's response surprises her.

'Is he shy or something?'

'Possibly. He tells me he has no ambition, not in the hotel trade anyway. Where do you think such a man's interest lies?'

The question sounds to him like a psychologist's professional wariness in the presence of a subject who might be unpredictable, even violent. He moves towards his greatcoat, which is hanging from a hook on the back of the door, and reaches for the pipe and tobacco in one of its deep pockets. But he believes his action might be a signal for behaviour she will recognise, so he disappoints her by picking up the hairbrush instead and bidding her to resume her seat in front of the mirror.

'I haven't finished,' he says, starting to draw the brush through the hair on the right side of her head. 'I don't know whether I want to know more of our Lorenz than I do at the moment. We're all just knuckling down here, finding our way.'

'Oh, come on! It's a new world. Anything goes.'

Bobby feels there is a sense in which almost everything Greta says applies only to herself and whoever else she thinks is like-minded. He wonders when he will be released from the memory of war to join her in a future she has already embraced. It will take a while. But he is not ready to tell her that he has watched Lorenz diving expertly into the hotel swimming pool without a splash and wondered why such accomplishment has to be subordinated to menial service. Perhaps she knows, or suspects. Perhaps Lorenz, not she, will be the one to give him swimming lessons.

'There,' he says. 'All done.'

She runs her hands through her hair and looks up at him. He seems vulnerable. She rises from the chair and touches his cheek, waiting for something to ensue. All that happens is that they gaze at each other. Then he kisses her on the forehead, as a father might kiss a daughter who has made him proud. But she pulls him towards her. Their lips clash then move apart before touching again, gently. Her mouth is open, as though she is about to express some feeling hovering between tenderness and indelicacy. They part, and she leaves the room feeling like a conspirator and having accomplished something.

He turns off the light and goes to the window. Having not seen the smoking guests, he watches Mr Kesselman re-occupy the empty space he left earlier, now succumbed to nightfall, and ponders the image of a man who has emerged from some indeterminate place to assume his allotted position. This evening, Mr Kesselman will join them in the main dining-room, where his vanity will shield him from the knowing glances behind his back.

Out on the lake, a boat begins nosing through a spread of glitter. The future, Greta always says, will be bright, and on the water it is signalled in all its faraway brilliance.

The Lister Building

Dear Charley,

By the time you read this I shall have made quite a mess of the Prime Minister. Not strictly true, as you well know, but I have observed Doctor Ferbusch long and often enough to have felt that it is I who am making those sleek wounds rather than he, the sad, pompous toosh. I am not supposed to let on that it is the PM who is to be wheeled before us tomorrow. We have been sworn to special secrecy, such as it is in in Room 24, where Doctor Ferbusch seeks the means of startling medical science with the pre-arranged complicity of the dead. Doctor Ferbusch once said to me, without looking up and therefore as though he were addressing the corpse itself in the manner of an apologist: 'A cadaver, Morley, is the supreme example of repose, and we should do as little as possible to disturb it.' To his credit, he achieves this – by straight, silent carving, the deft leafing of tissue, the reverential transfer of organs *in vitro* and, I have to say, a fearsome responsibility where his vocation is concerned.

The PM is what we call 'a Quality Bod' or 'QB', and this is the closest we sail to levity. As you can appreciate, 'QBs' are pretty rare around here, perhaps because, in life, celebrity confers a certain loathing of proximity combined with a fear of decline. (Is it shallow to display irritation at Doctor Ferbusch's habit of always calling me 'Morley'?) Anyway, the last 'QB' we had in was a former Admiral of the Fleet with a liver the size of a jellyfish. I almost threw up (those were the early days) which was odd considering that the aura of eternal rest with which the dead confront us nearly always settles my stomach. I say 'almost', but there was an instant on that occasion when my own body hovered between revulsion and merriment: I formed a picture of a mariner who had been transformed by his element into something mythic, and I began to wonder whether or not Doctor Ferbusch would start hauling out halibut lungs, conger entrails and stiff, salt-plugged veins! But then I glimpsed a word – seafarer – passing along the great waters of thought and I assumed Doctor Ferbusch's studied calm. Seafarer.

Before I leave all this for a moment, dear Charley, I must mention Doctor Ferbusch's little secret, no longer such. It all began a few weeks ago when I answered the phone to Mrs Ferbusch. Whether she was scatty or beside herself, even deaf, or whether it was my sore throat, or a combination of all these, she evidently mistook me for her husband, who was dealing with something down the corridor. Before I could explain that it was really me, Peter Morley the lab technician, she spluttered: 'Enough is enough. I rang the clinic myself if you must know and they said you hadn't been there. Good god – you're a doctor yourself; you should realise

81

what's wrong with you, if anything!' And with that she slammed down the receiver. Seconds later I heard the squelch of Doctor Ferbusch's shoes on the polished floor. As he entered the room, my frozen features obviously puzzled him.

'What's up, Morley?' he asked. 'Seen a ghost?' (Away from the dissecting table, Doctor Ferbusch is not without a sense of humour.)

'It was Mrs Ferbusch,' I explained. 'On the phone. She seemed upset.' He looked at me with the expression of a trusting parent who has probably been told a fib and feels both injured and resentful. He called his wife immediately while I shuffled some glinting tools of the trade in a neutral corner with my back to him. I heard my name mentioned. I was trying not to listen by making as much rattle as seemed discreet.

We had just sewn up a sunken party from Faversham, a Mr Proudfoot (honest!!), and the undertaker had already collected, leaving behind certain essential organs which had come to rest in their jars and awaited further examination in a remoter place we minions call the Eureka Temple. We neither hear the cries of discovery from there nor receive credit for having to pickpocket our clients in the first place. Doctor Ferbusch is our only link with both zones. He sees the job through, filleting in 24 then slicing microscopically in Eureka. He was due there that afternoon but had been taking an inordinately long time to scrub up at the sink. He began to speak. His words seemed to strike the wall in front of him and sky across to me as I deliberately set imaginary dinner-places. 'Did you get her drift, Morley?' he asked. I paused as though I hadn't heard or was weighing what he had said, and then I replied: 'Not really, Doctor Ferbusch. Are you ill?

Is there anything I can do?' He was curt. 'No there isn't, Morley,' he said. 'Just stitch your lip, if you will.' I was reminded of an aristocrat's being forced to speak to the lower orders against his better judgement. Getting rid of me would have been no solution: it would simply have accelerated gossip.

In any case, we have come to share much, Doctor Ferbusch and I. We occupy the bleached quarters of the afterlife; we are the unacknowledged mutilators; and now we are bonded anew by something unspoken, something growing inside Doctor Ferbusch himself, like an incipient surprise. For I have seen him falter of late as one does when, outside Sainsbury's, comes the realisation that the contents of one's bag do not match the memorised shopping-list with which one strode so confidently into the store, and a trivial lapse appears for a second to be momentous.

But this may have been over-excitement, because Major-General F----------, a stout JP from Guildford, looking up at us with indestructible reproach (we re-open their eyes), was a twin, and Doctor Ferbusch has been assured of access to the body of the survivor. Perhaps he was contemplating fame, an article in *The Lancet* with photographs of the twins laid out side by side like a pair of identical Bacchi. Somehow, though, I don't think Doctor Ferbusch is one for wine and merriment. He sermonises ('Learn something from this, Morley.'). He is stern. Just the chap to take the smile off the PM's face with a blade. But more of that in a minute.

Charley, I miss you. It still haunts me, that image of the two of us heading into the storm on Highgate Hill, with the Whittington shining ahead, a beacon on some transported Edwardian evening. Then the classes we went to, the

Polaroid of little Ben writhing inside you – a starscape, one vast constellation reordering itself into an infant's shape – and our knowledge that Ben was not mine, and the moment when our provisional moorings slipped and we began our tearful, separate drifting into the night. I sometimes look across at Doctor Ferbusch and wonder if he has anyone like you, anyone at a distance, shedding with time all the ugliness of the spirit. I don't suppose you hear anything of Nick. Doctor Ferbusch was glad to see the back of him – figuratively speaking, of course! Doctor Ferbusch demands so much concentration on detail that he likened the tension between me and Nick to that generated by a pair of animals tugging at opposite ends of a metal bar. It was Nick, wasn't it? After his first couple of days here, Doctor Ferbusch asked me, 'Well, Morley – what do you think of the new pair of hands?' I couldn't say one way or the other, but Doctor Ferbusch, having sliced, probed and sewn, said simply, 'A ladies' man'.

After Nick left, on a day when Doctor Ferbusch had been more than routinely jovial while bearing down on a breastbone, I began to receive the cool, restorative Ferbusch treatment. With a tuck here and a nip there, he began patching me up. 'Who's Charlotte?' he had asked once, when we were three. Nick and I stared at each other, a mere stride separating us between head and toe of an Oxford don, a Dr Beatrice something-or-other, her silver hair still done up with ancient clips. 'She rang,' he said. 'Apparently, either of you will do.' Then later, I suppose after he thought was a decent interval, he began talking about disengagement. 'Do you believe in the soul, Morley?' he would ask. Maybe it was a celebration of Nick's departure.

Shortly afterwards he told me about his sarcoma. He was so objective, it sounded like a cat he'd taken in, a cat which, though unruly, had attached itself to him with a passion quite beyond his control. Did Nick ever tell you that it was he who had done the pregnancy test on the sample you gave me? He'd returned to the Path Lab by then. I was with him in that room with the twelve-foot preserved tapeworm in its Perspex tunnel, when he injected the midwife toads, calling me a few days later to view them as they kicked and bulged with eggs in dumb proclamation of your motherhood.

Doctor Ferbusch was not amused to think that Nick and I were involved with the same woman. Nick's leaving restored his moral certainty. Doctor Ferbusch has dwelt so long amidst the un-imagining flesh that he is as contemptuous of life as those who believe there is brighter and better to come. Immersed in his bluff landscapes of disfigurement, he will say something like, 'All that intrigue, Morley, just for this', as if dying were the whole point of living. He was right about Nick, but in a way that must always make the recipients of that kind of observation feel ever so slightly inferior: out of the race, as it were, or even a non-runner. I have increased in stature, Nick's flippancy having made my surly cleverness seem like something Doctor Ferbusch might turn to advantage. He has always been filled with pleasure and a superior pride to see someone dabbling at the edge of the thicket of learning in which all that can be seen of him is his bent back. For a while now, he has been bringing in obscure journals, which lie around like copies of *National Geographic* in a dentist's surgery. In one I discovered a piece called 'Guillan-Barre Syndrome: Early Descriptions of Ascending Paralysis' (I'm into syndromes, as you'll see). There were grainy pictures of Guillan at Salpetriere, standing next to the dissector like Proust with a Metropol chef before the neat carving of livers.

I couldn't help making the connection between those odd men at the frontiers of research, tracing a phantom immobiliser as it spread cell by cell through the body then just as strangely reversing itself like the receding ice of spring, with those nights when your hands quietly palmed away my delirium and pacified for a while the rebellion in my glands, leaving me with memories of what seemed like a divine visitation. Your friend was right: I have contracted Exupéry's Syndrome. It's like Guillan-Barre but more emotional than physical. 'Contracted' – it sounds like a pact. Even as you fondled me I was regressing. In my body, the masculine side is temporarily in decline, leaving the feminine one in the ascendant for a while at least. It's a rare condition. I'm almost a girl. Did you notice? Could you feel anything? Was I different? I voyage temporarily in a woman's province. I ought to feel privileged. Dr Ferbusch would be delighted, at the proper time, to cut me up! Anyway, how are you enjoying Australia? Is it far enough away from both the fickle male (Nick) and the reluctant one (me)?

I'm writing this at night. It is very late. Outside the window, London glows and wails. They asked me if I'd suffered any shock. (Apparently, trauma can set Exupéry's in motion: I think of it as 'Exuberance', something deserved after misery, after a fright to the system.) I didn't tell them exactly what I do as a Lab Technician Grade 2, but I'm fascinated more than horrified by the idea that Doctor Ferbusch's first, ventral puncture in my presence may have started an endocrine revolt inside me. I remember it well, though some of the intervening donors between that and tomorrow's *coup de théâtre* no longer register. It was a Mr Purser, an elderly cove from St Leonard's. (Most of them have had a good slog: you don't think about offering your body for research until intimations of mortality grow benign.) I recall that his face wore the twitch of a grin. Doctor Ferbusch said, 'Look at this, Morley. Bet he's never bought a round in his life', Doctor Ferbusch's idea of stinginess being signalled by a beam of self-satisfaction. Purser was in good working order, so most of him had to come out, the weighty stuff as well as the hidden pearls.

You don't know this, but not long ago I started holding the hand of the corpse. I felt like a prodigal offering belated contrition to a parent whose capacity for forgiveness had expired. I looked down on humanity and wondered at the body's ability to astound with the intricacy of its once-palpitating bits and pieces. I'm sure Doctor Ferbsuch thinks this way; it's just that, until now, he has not brought himself to acknowledge what the subjects set before him tell us so plainly. (Nick likened Doctor Ferbusch at work to a diner nitpicking at a hearty meal.) Tomorrow, the occasion just might get the better of him and he will begin, ever so cautiously, to treat me as an equal.

You should have seen the PM's obituaries. Two whole pages in *The Times*, like an advert for one of those boring Pacific island dictatorships, with the smiling portrait we have all confronted so often. Such a busy committed individual, and so unavailing in my case. Doctor Ferbusch has always been a big fan and considers it an honour to be expediting the final wish, buried in the obit's penultimate paragraph to clinch the case, if argument were needed, for a sweeping public-spiritedness. Doctor Ferbusch wasn't obliged to identify our special guest until the actual unveiling. As it was, he left it until the last minute, so that I arrived home tonight in a daze and feeling not a tad privileged. Thus, I have not seen the PM prostrate and ivory-white, but I know exactly where he is, at what temperature he lies and which light washes the folds of his shroud with colour as the generator whirrs mysteriously.

Dear Charley, we are all on the move in one way or another. Nick has grown quite tubby on examination success in Pathology and frolics with a harem of 'girls'. Did you know that a median ventral incision from Adam's apple to belly-button leaves behind the faintest streak of blood, or a black mark that used to be blood? It's like a jet stream except that the deceased will no longer make the journey it signifies; unlike the ones we can see being made in the skylight, the vapour trails leading to safer havens far away.

Ah well, the shadows of the living play fitfully on the brows of the dead. For a while, anyway.

Yours wherever and whenever, and with some trepidation,

Peter

Uncle Kaiser

Arundel Square, Islington

Ever since that skinhead made my eyes water with his flamethrower breath, I'd wanted to find out about Johnny Harn. This was because I am a clever dick. Or so my Uncle Kaiser told everyone. He was pretty sharp, too. Other members of the family, huddling in their darkened havens, pleaded with us to make simpler connections. Even the sight of a white man running along the pavement scares them.

I could say that I had been minding my own business if my business did not offer up a scent to the hunters with the lolling tongues. Two of them fell out of a car last week and strode towards me in that earnest gait of theirs. Then one grabbed me, scrunched his face close to mine and said: 'Fuck off to the fucking jungle fucking Paki shit-shoveller!'

It's the physique of these men which impresses me. That, and the ferocity of what motivates them. They sometimes remind me of goblins on white chargers. And they are, of course, the heirs of Johnny Harn, in the 1930s an Oswald

Mosley Blackshirt, though they'd probably have knocked him off the pavement if he'd got in their way. Harn was in his eighties. He was old and grey, as they say, but still walked the streets, as if still looking for trouble, for undying grief. Oh that mischief would die with the mischief-makers! Uncle Kaiser was obsessed by him, though they'd never met. At the end, I think my uncle wanted to meet him, shake his hand, erase the past and dissolve into the future. But it's not all over. He has spawned them and my kind has spawned me and we eye each other across the road, a no-man's-land.

Redman's Road, Stepney

Uncle Kaiser was sizing me up in the bedroom of his council flat near Stepney Green. He'd called me over for something and told me to sit in the window, just behind the curtain. It was the usual Saturday morning bustle in the street below. He told me to keep looking. But I could sense him watching me. Watching me looking for Johnny Harn.

'Give him five minutes,' he said. 'Harn always shows.'

Five minutes of bronchial music behind me. Then a figure appears, someone I'd never seen before but strangely distinctive, a presence, shuffling almost, and carrying a Tesco's bag.

'This him?'

'Describe what you see.'

'Smartish old man, white hair with Foreign Legion cut, and...'

'What?'

'Sort of bent up.'

'Curvature of the spine. Old age ramming home its message.'

The Juniper Hotel, Bombay

It was always the British who were so exasperated. Heirs to a fierce decorum, they hopped off the planes and marched towards Uncle Kaiser at Reception. He would smile at the race between a guest and an advanced booking. The guest invariably won.

'But we sent a telegram four days ago.'

'No telegram, sir.'

'Impossible.'

'Telegram delayed, perhaps?'

'Delayed? Now look here, that's a bloody contradiction in terms. Where's the manager?'

Uncle Kaiser aspired to management. He had two white shirts. Each night he dabbed the collars with tennis-shoe cream.

'Manager at big meeting in Khalnapoor, sir.'

I imagined Uncle Kaiser standing to attention amid the smell of disinfectant and spices, obedient to an imported habit of unflappability. This was not necessary with the journalists and the *voyageurs sauvages*. He once heard them talking about the emptying of bowels on the Khalnapoor road. It appeared that a family of six were crouched together beside the railway, bobbing up and down in unison. 'India is a big country,' he told them, to justify his contempt for latrines. 'India can take it.'

Redman's Road, Stepney

Uncle Kaiser was a life member of the cut-and-pummelled brigade. He once showed me a story he had written for *The Golden Bridge*, a publication in Urdu. In the story, Bhata, a London bus conductor (you see how old this is), spots a white bullock in Marylebone Road and dashes out to control the traffic. A common theme, Uncle Kaiser said, the urge to do one's best for a proud dislocation.

Bhata, it seemed, led the bullock away through staring crowds, unaware of how stupid he looked.

'You see,' said Uncle Kaiser. 'Inside, this Bhata is clean, so nothing can harm him. This filth, this oppression, is maya, illusion.'

'Harn's strictly second division,' I suggested. 'No hope of sainthood, surely.'

'Don't you believe it. They need people like Harn to change the tune, modulate it, supply new hateful choruses. Harn was a Mosley lieutenant, a boot boy. But he's survived. So they look up to him, the younger ones.'

The Juniper Hotel, Bombay

E.M. Forster was much discussed at reception, particularly among the British journalists, of whom Mary Hunter was one.

'Anyone who marries an Indian marries half the country,' Uncle Kaiser told them. 'That Miss Quested – she knew what was what but chickened out. Now Mrs Moore was something else. She could have handled the scale of things earlier in life.'

Uncle Kaiser was sure Mary Hunter understood. He learned from her that Britain was small, its clans circumscribed. In order to impress her, he went for the assistant manager's job at the Lake Prospect. Sometimes they walked hand in hand to watch the waters lapping India.

Chowpatti Beach, Bombay

Mary Hunter had no problems of adjustment in Uncle Kaiser's country. She did not even experience that symmetrical swing of the emotions suffered by expatriates at The Juniper, which begins with wonder, progresses to doubt and terminates in revulsion. Uncle Kaiser was the epitome of optimism. He would stand at the water's edge and quote some obscure Himalayan hermit-philosopher on patent evidence of the eternal. The sea affirmed it. Yet he and Mary Hunter had both seen through the myth of spirituality in that land. Spirit of place, spirit of the wild, spirit of irrationality. Uncle Kaiser's dismay lay in the contemplation of the ruins of fantasy. 'In a country of such abundance, it is easy to do little,' he would say. 'So the great become inherently good. Our sin is that we know this but still do nothing.'

Redman's Road, Stepney

Uncle Kaiser was keen on history in which he had been involved. When he told me this I immediately thought of the Independence movement, but he did not consider that being part of those waves of dissent in the dust counted, at least not in a personal way.

'I was thinking more of one's role as direct victim,' he explained. 'When we came over, Mosley's legatees had lost interest in the Jews. I always pictured them sneering at usury then looking over their shoulders at this commotion in the docks – once, then twice for a long stare, open-mouthed, at another shock to their system. The Blacks. People like Harn were delegated to provide the amended rationale for hatred. But Harn has always been anti-Semitic. You sometimes see letters from him in the *Courier*, going on about Central European businessmen who change their names to dignify the making of fortunes. He means the Jews, you see. Englishmen have forgotten this. They've also forgotten that names no longer need to be changed.'

Uncle Kaiser loved to prove that exceptional acts were nothing of the sort. Swamped by the clutter of his room, he looked bohemian. I suppose he was a sort of artist. He'd written 'filler pars' for the Indian newspapers.

Lake Prospect Hotel, Bombay

Uncle Kaiser now had his own office. It was not far from a new Reception but it had a window with a view of the Raj University. In that room he discovered solitude, or the means of its refinement, the redeeming pleasure of exclusion. Mr Singh, the manager, was not only forbidden by the caste system to share a table with him but, like all members of a privileged group, went out of his way to maintain the divide, letting go only when Mary Hunter came visiting.

'I hear the membership rule is to be relaxed at the Bridge Club,' he once said in a rapid-fire voice, tightening the knot in his tie as though he had been recommended for membership and was about to answer a summons from the vetting committee.

Uncle Kaiser, amused by Mr Singh's excitement at the waiving of a regulation, raised his eyebrows at Mary Hunter, inviting her to put Mr Singh out of his misery, one way or another.

'I think not,' she said. 'Though there is talk.'

Mr Singh's face registered sadness at this postponement of *entrée*. Then he left.

'What fun!' Uncle Kaiser exclaimed. 'The Raj builds its Bombay piles after its own fashion, thus insulting the society in which they are to stand, yet adopts the same society's most obnoxious convention in order to preserve its integrity. Perhaps it should not stop there. Perhaps its womenfolk should set fire to themselves when their husbands die. This also is custom.'

In his office, Uncle Kaiser began reading about Hampton Court, the British Museum, the Tower of London.

Rillington Place, Notting Hill

Ostracism killed Mary Hunter, according to Uncle Kaiser.

'She was philosophical about it,' he said. 'But one should never underestimate the English capacity for narrow-mindedness behind that liberal exterior. I personally have always been shit-scared of bulldogs. And rightly so.'

Ealing, where Mary's parents lived, was probably

untainted then by the veil of sleaziness which London has draped over itself. Old man Hunter, ravaged by war service, and Mrs Hunter, seared by proximity to the thought of invasion, were indifferent to their daughter's marriage to Uncle Kaiser and rarely visited the house the couple rented three doors down from John Christie, then stashing away women's bodies behind the walls of No.10. There were rows.

'What is your pain to the deaths of so many?' Uncle Kaiser had once shouted at her, referring not to the unsuspecting who clicked along the pavement for Mr Christie's quack remedies but the subcontinent's unremembered vales of suffering. It was bowel cancer. Uncle Kaiser wept two stones in six months. 'To think I knew Christie,' he would say later. 'A smiling man, with a name so close to the celestial. A man in a cardigan, clipping the hedge.'

Arundel Square, Islington

Thus did Mary Hunter experience Purdah.

N.R. Gaffur described the symbolism in Uncle Kaiser's stories as 'a tart's jewellery'. This was clever, too, as Uncle Kaiser himself conceded, by sniping at the parts cleverly one could condemn the whole without elaboration. Coming from a Hindu critic based in London this effectively did for Uncle Kaiser in his efforts to munch on the lowland pastures of English letters.

And it really is difficult not to see everything as portent when migration is so frustrated. Uncle Kaiser's brother, my father, also married an Englishwoman. So here, between shrill Boat people and senile cockneys, between an appeal and its rebuttal locked in everlasting embrace, I stared at the mirror and saw a flame-coloured symbol of division against a strange drama enacted in a park opposite. A man entices a Staffordshire bull terrier to chew on an Arsenal scarf, then ties the scarf to the branch of a tree, almost out of the dog's reach but not quite. The man sits on a bench to read his newspaper as the dog makes more and more frantic efforts to grab the end of the suspended scarf, which it eventually does, hanging there, spinning, in mid-air.

'The front line is everywhere,' Uncle Kaiser said. 'Only one world is surveyed by those in a state of battle-readiness.' In Uncle Kaiser's case, it was fatigue but the images were no less potent. 'Did you know that Johnny Harn served in India?' he asked me. Uncle Kaiser had done his homework on Harn. For years he had been in crazy orbit around him.

Redman's Road, Stepney

A man with bronchitis is a man attracting attention to himself.

Street lamps bathed Uncle Kaiser's flat in a cinematic half-light, enhanced when he drew deeply on his cigarettes.

'I think I may beat Johnny Harn to the East London Crematorium,' he said.

'Why don't you give up smoking, then?'

'Too late.'

'It's only too late if you've got something terminal, such as curvature of the spine.'

He tried to pass off a cough as a laugh.

'If I go first, ask the superintendent how it was that the

telegram from the Maker insisting on the survival of the ill-used over the tyrant never arrived. Tell him the non-arrival of such a message is a contradiction in terms.'

In the final weeks he talked a lot about marching: Gandhi's Salt Trek, Mosley's Blackshirts in Cable Street, the column of exasperated guests at the Juniper, the trek from Auschwitz to Bergen-Belsen, Johnny Harn and his Union Movement chums in Notting Hill, refugees everywhere in flight. I was at the flat when he died. It was several minutes before I realised that the furtive wheezing had stopped. As I brushed the palm of my hand across his eyes, like they do in films, an anonymous white male with four lungs called to someone on the other side of the city and the great bellowing arc clasped the night in a steel girdle. I thought of the world as it is. It is one world. As we see it is as it is. I thought of minarets and their wailing calls to prayer.

East London Crematorium

Uncle Kaiser's books and paperwork came to me – *Howard's End*, *Victorian Love Poetry*, the *Magazine Writers' Journal* – along with the scrapbooks, one of them chronicling his wrinkled testimony to advancement, which started with an account of prize-distribution day at Bombay's Kishan-garh Mission in 1936 and ended with 'City Slicker', his contribution to *The Golden Bridge*, next to which was pasted Gaffur's withering review like a death sentence. Uncle Kaiser wasn't all that good as a literary hombre. In another scrapbook I saw a picture of a rod-stiff John Harn on parade with Mosley, each with the face of someone about to bite a lump out of the photographer's head.

Not even fascists, I guessed, would register more than a scowl at the sight of a 'Paki' in a place like that. In any case, I was well hidden among the spectres of the determinedly bereaved as Harn's coffin was tilted on to a trolley and wheeled towards the conveyor belt. How do they do it? I almost spoke out loud. How do they pack a man into a casket who has changed shape from a snarling exclamation to a timid question mark barely able to support itself? Another item of lame symbolism, as Mr Gaffur might have spotted, yet typical of Uncle Kaiser as wishful thinker. There was enough gorilla support among the bearers to have shouldered that figurative change of heart. The strains of 'Abide With Me' seeped out, like thin blood. Then they burned him. Then he became one with all raddled occupants of the pyre.

Grasmere

'If he comes, he comes; if not...'

Millie's sentence trails away from its opening words, which remind her of a childhood game, the one where a name or a phrase is repeated over and over until gradually it loses its meaning and becomes a mantra with a new, undisclosed power.

They are renting a house by the lake, she and Carl and Ziggy, their daughter. 'Ziggy' was Carl's choice, something he saw in a newspaper report about a rock star and her husband with their first-born. She mostly goes along with Carl's suggestions, not out of indifference but from a need to let someone else rebel for her. In darker moments, she puts this down to a lack of imagination, a willingness to be led. One of her primary school teachers said as much in an end-of-year report – 'Millie is a bright pupil but she allows herself to be influenced unduly by others.'

This holiday is out of season, out of the ordinary. The lake waters at the bottom of the garden support a flotilla of upturned leaves, like some Venetian festival seen from afar.

The crowd is waving its coat-tails at late autumn. The trees have turned ink-black and gulls are swinging in from a heaving sea.

'If he comes, he comes,' she says. 'If not...'

'If not, it won't make a blind bit of difference,' Carl says eventually, spreading a map beside the Sunday paper on the floor as though he is a platoon commander. Ziggy is in front of the log fire, looking for nits in the hair of a rag doll.

'I never know whether you are being resentful or innocent,' Millie says.

She is at the window, away from the other two. The mist has dropped a crown on the summit of the high fell across the water. Her breath is condensing for a mini-second on the windowpane.

'What are you doing?' he asks.

'I was thinking of that test which is supposed to tell whether you are an optimist or a pessimist – is a bottle half full of water or half empty? Is the condensation trying to take over or is it being repelled by the flames?'

She breathes gently again, this time prolonging the motion so that she has time to make her fingerprint before it goes away, like a quiet death. Luke is flying over from Paris and might already be in the country, on his way to them via the Midlands and the M6.

'He said he'd come,' she states, a little petulantly. 'Or try to.'

'There's no telling with Luke. Perhaps he'll phone, perhaps not. Let's just enjoy ourselves, shall we?'

'I want to feed the ducks,' Millie interrupts, the resident doll now limp in the fireplace, discarded by yet another foster parent. She is struggling to put on her padded jacket with the hood, a miniature version of her mother's. Carl takes no notice. His finger is moving north from Windermere to Ambleside, then east to the Langland valley. The map crinkles beneath its advance.

'I'll take you,' Millie says, without turning towards them. 'We'll scrunch up some bread.'

Carl folds the map. Seconds later, he can hear the two of them in the kitchen: Ziggy the interrogator and Millie the woman with the answers to questions about ducks – where they come from, where they go, who feeds them when there's no-one at the house, what they do at night. He lets them get on with it, then follows them to the lake's edge and watches them scattering the crumbs on the water. Ziggy's handfuls fall short on the pebbly shore. Millie kneels down to retrieve the bits. As her head lowers, the lake comes up to meet her and she realises the waters are lapping almost imperceptibly at her feet. It reminds her of someone whispering. Only down there, close to it, away from Carl, can she be privy to its message. Without dipping her fingers, she senses the water's cold. Something about its clarity, the absence of muddying life, the precious stones waving under the ripples, tell her so.

'Here they come,' Carl says.

The ducks have been swimming anonymously offshore, but are now heading towards them in V-formation. They are all dowdy females. One day soon, Millie thinks, Ziggy will want to know how a brace of mallards hanging from a butcher's hook like aristocrats' capes on a peg have met their fate. Ziggy will not comment on the explanation, just stare, seemingly at the inevitable. Just as Luke once did.

Millie sees so much of Luke in Ziggy. And the more Carl

learns about Luke the more Ziggy seems to him to be forming in her uncle's image. There is a baby grand piano in a room built on to the side of the house, its dull walnut camouflage merging into the shadows. But the room is locked. They saw the advert for the house in the *Sunday Times*. Millie swears she didn't know about the piano, which Carl thinks is probably true because there are other indicators of a house leased conditionally – tacit messages of prohibition – such as a drinks cupboard and an expensive hi-fi also barred. Not that Luke now plays much in company, even for his own uncomprehending family.

Luke at the piano, fingers blurring across the keyboard. That's what most people remember. A musician in full flow. But Millie liked it when he hunched himself over the keys, inspecting his fingers at close quarters as they printed a meditative chain of chords on the air. Words were like chords: both consisted of merged blocks of meaning. There are just two years between them. They did everything together, including learn to play the piano, but in most cases Luke out distanced her, especially as a musician. While she, Carl and Ziggy were eating at motorway services earlier that day, a television was showing the advert in which toy bunnies powered by different makes of battery fall by the wayside until the fittest bunny overtakes the last powerless competitor and goes running on for eternity. She suddenly recalled the muffled sounds of Liszt, Chopin and Rachmaninov coming from the front room at home: Luke powering on to his Grade Eight as she remained mute, her interest and ability spent. She rarely went in to see him. The picture she retains is by proxy, an urchin in short trousers, his feet dangling from the piano stool in that now grainy documentary the BBC made about him and a few other, unrelated, prodigies. It all turned out to be sad and it was sad at the time in a strange sort of way.

The ducks are frenzy feeding at two locations – one controlled by Carl, who is standing a few yards away, and the other by Millie and Ziggy, crouching head to head. Ziggy fancies she can see herself reflected in the ducks' eyes.

'Do you think he'll arrive today?' Carl asks. He is watching the cars on the lakeside road opposite, the only road, beyond the central wooded island. Some are turning into the village, others motoring on to Keswick and points in between. He often wondered what the locals did when the roads became snowbound. Just waited, he supposed.

'Maybe. You know Luke. Today, tomorrow – whenever.'

Carl picks up a disc-shaped pebble and skims it across the water. Luke's visits are infrequent but they always make Carl miserable. Perhaps it's because all rare visits are, by definition, badly timed. Some other day or weekend is always preferable or more convenient; some excuse for postponement always at hand. These days all their spare time seems to be occluded by others, even people they are delighted to see when they know the delight will only be appreciated at the time and in retrospect. Luke does all the things that Carl does – watches TV trash, drinks beer at the pub, talks about sport – but Carl always feels something is being kept from him to do with the realm Luke occupies, however reluctantly. What is worse, Carl wonders, being part of a dominion or harbouring the resentments of exile? These are Carl's words. Carl is not bound by men's talk. Millie tells him he impresses Luke but he doesn't believe it. Another stone, this one plumbing straight to the bottom.

'I want to go to the gingerbread shop now,' Ziggy says, as the ducks start to lose interest. 'And then I want to see the lion and the lamb.'

'You can see the lion and the lamb from here,' Carl says, turning his back on the lake.

He looks up at the peak to the north of the village and searches for its whimsical outcrop. But the sun is momentarily blinding. He once lugged camera equipment to the spot for a five-minute scene in a film about the painter Kurt Schwitters, who lived for a while, and incongruously, in Ambleside. Perhaps because they had both been at different times on opposite sides of a TV camera, he tried to interest Luke in Schwitters, making the point that the discordant notes in the painter's collages were musical, only for Luke to counter that no-one ever made the comparison for concordant images. Carl felt this meant that Luke thought him unmusical in the sense that only the negative view of art exercised those who had no real interest in it: the 'I Know What I Like' school, its adherents too much on the defensive to be interested in even their own entrenched positions. Luke was argumentative when he wasn't sullen or ironic. Or elsewhere.

Carl can feel Ziggy tugging at his coat. She insists on the gingerbread shop. It will still be open, its little jaw muscles aching before autumn's trickle of tourists. Above them, a black cloud over Silver Howe is about to advance on the sun.

They bypass the churchyard, where the plain tombstones of the Wordsworths are crowded in a corner like the markers of plague victims. Whenever Millie goes there, along the signposted path, she never stops but instead allows her fingers to run along the top of the iron fence, to feel its snagging scales of rust and the faint communication of pain beneath curative layers of paint.

'It's not our first visit,' Millie tells the gingerbread woman. 'We used to come with rucksacks when we were younger and we've brought Ziggy three times, haven't we Ziggy?'

The woman half-smiles at the child, as though curious about the relationships in front of her.

'The weather has never been fine for long,' Millie continues. 'Perhaps we come at the wrong time.' She recalls a few clear days followed by fog or gentle, restorative drizzle, through which the mountains stood like monstrous presences.

More clouds are heading north so they decide to return. Ziggy is half asleep. Carl will normally drag her along rather than give in and carry her. She is heavy. But he relents. Next to his face her woollen jumper smells of stale bread and things she's eaten in the previous two hours – prawn-flavoured Skips, liquorice wheels, chocolate. He thinks about the resilience of a child's tummy.

As they round the corner near the garden centre, the house can be seen in the distance. Millie notices that theirs is still the only car parked alongside. It will be two weeks before the clocks go back, yet the dark evenings are already in place, moving on, with clock-watching humanity in tow, its arms outstretched.

Inside the house, Carl says no more about Luke. He removes the guard from the fireplace and stokes the logs. The sudden crackle lights up their faces. Ziggy is asleep on the settee, imitating a rag doll.

'I'll take her up,' he says presently. 'Then I think I'll turn in myself. What about you?'

'I'll watch the fire die down. You go on.'

They needn't have lit a fire because the central heating is on all the time. It is just that Carl always does so whenever they stay in the Lakes, whenever there is a hoard of logs outside under a corrugated tin roof. Carl was once a Cub Scout, a sixer; Millie sometimes imagines him in short trousers and socks, with his green tabs sticking out below his knees like gold leaf raised by static electricity. Tiny pennants of flame issue now and then from fissures in the burnt wood. Millie sees them as pockets of resistance in some blazing conflict long decided. They hiss, snap for a moment, then are vanquished, unlike the patterns in the wood itself, those whorls, knots and ladders which have come through or been transformed by the dark. It is a cold land that has been laid waste and in it she becomes aware of the warmth of her own body, the sense of her shaping nakedness. Curled up on the chair, she feels hugely accommodating and wriggles into a provocative position, her legs apart. This has nothing to do with Carl. This is the domain she craves, her own warmth igniting things, having an influence. She turns towards the dying fire and coils her tongue round a loose strand of hair. It is night-time in the Lakes, when fellside lights burn with solitary cheerlessness and the past re-establishes itself noiselessly like the tide filling a shadowy creek. At motorway services she bought a wad of miniature Penguin paperbacks – Melville's *Bartleby*; Goethe's *Letters from Italy*; and the dirty stories of Anais Nin, the commission of a nameless voyeur. Carl will not approve of this last, but if he happens to pick it up and remonstrate with her she will probably feign innocence, as though it was something that crept unknowingly into the pile. He never reads her books, so they never fight over who will be the first to settle down with one. But she scans the first story, 'The Woman on the Dunes'. It reminds her of a tinkling accompaniment to pleasure that is also its source, a paradigm of seduction.

She hears a faint bump behind her. Ziggy is standing in the doorway. She has padded downstairs without the landing light on and is rubbing her right eye with the hem of her nightie.

'Are the ducks in?' she asks, sleepily.

'The ducks are on the water, sweetheart, where we left them.'

'I want to see them again.'

'It's a bit late, and cold. You should be asleep.'

Ziggy picks up her jacket from the chair.

'OK,' Millie says. 'Just for five minutes.' She puts on her own jacket, dips her feet into her slippers and makes a crucifix with her forefinger and lips to crave silence before lifting the latch on the back door.

It isn't cold at all outside, and there is a taste of water on her tongue, earthy and mineral. She carries Ziggy across the strand of pebbles, stepping gingerly so as not to make a noise. Ziggy looks ahead and frowns, as if at some remnant of a dream. They are almost at the edge when the noise of splashing reaches them, a trail of surface slaps on the water that they can now see catching some hidden night light, perhaps from the moon lodged behind thick cloud. They look like prints, each with its tiny commotion of wavelets, and then at their head they see a duck treading the air before its wings begin beating their frantic message of flight. As children, staring into the bedroom's dark, Millie and Luke would sit enthralled as objects issued slowly out of their background like things coming into being. Luke always saw them first. 'Tallboy!' he would snap, ahead of her.

Ziggy wants to go further down the lakeside, away from the house. Millie looks back as they walk. Carl has not stirred. Moonlight picks out their car, which shines as if naturally luminous. Ziggy wants to see more ducks. The light that makes their car glow now settles on the boulders in their path.

'Wait here,' Millie says, sitting down on one of them, suddenly feeling weary. 'It'll come back.'

'What will?'

It is a desultory question. Ziggy is walking in circles on the stones. Millie looks down. She can see that the pebbles are dry on top but seem to be embedded in water or damp sandy soil. She begins turning them over with her feet. They make a faint clacking sound.

'The duck, of course. What did you think?'

And far off, perhaps even as far away as neighbouring Rydal Water, they can hear the relentless flapping of wings. It is Ziggy who looks first. Before joining her, Millie sits staring at the upturned stones and the smaller ones exposed beneath them and the grains of sand still deeper. She cups the water, as if to drink; she knows it is only clear because it has been purged of life by acid rain.

Then they are both on their feet, straining excitedly as the noise grows louder, their gaze fixed on the sky above the light-dusted treetops, which meander between Grasmere and Rydal. Coming towards them, arrowing downwards, are two ducks, separated by the meanest of distances. They're racing each other, or the one is fleeing from its trailing partner, or the one behind is in pursuit of its victim. Drawing alongside, twenty feet above the water, they coast down, their urgent flapping done, and land together peaceably. Ziggy laughs at their self-congratulatory tail-wagging. It's all over.

'Time to go back,' Millie says. Ziggy agrees. A tired Ziggy never argues.

As they approach the house, a car in some sort of hurry comes racing up the lake road towards the house. But it passes after slowing. They can hear it on the side of the fell. Within seconds the mountain has enfolded it.

The clouds are moving now, like emissaries charged with an urgent mission, and leaves begin to drift against the French windows of the music room.

Mrs Kuroda on Penyfan

Solemn over fertile country floats the white cloud.

Mrs Kuroda remembered those words from the diary she had kept as a teenager, and now they seemed to be written in the skies, signalling to her personally a truth so long untold. In those days, she kept lots of similar things: newspaper cuttings, snippets from books, tattered pictures of the Western world. Each will come true, she had told herself, each will materialise.

Smithereens. She had learnt that word from Bill while they were underground at the mining museum. Ichiro, her husband, hadn't been bothered at all. 'Look after her, Bill,' he had said, emphasising the man's name as though he had been practising it all night for some important leave-taking ceremony at which his face would be creased, all-smiling. That was why he had done so well for himself, Mrs Kuroda thought. His determination to succeed in that windswept, hilly land among its emotional people would see them through. Forty years before, in Nagasaki, these were the qualities which mothers-to-be seemed to will on their unborn children in the anguish of bringing them into the world. Mothers who had survived, of course. 'Blown to smithereens,' Bill had said while recounting the tail of the pit disaster. It was almost as if Ichiro had instructed him to mention it, in order to impress on his wife the triumph of similarity over difference.

Alone in their house in the Vale, she stared at her face in the dressing-table mirror, vaguely aware of the double reflection looking in from its two side panels. In front of her was the photograph. The whole effect was that of a shrine, in which she and her mirror images were fixed; not the gazer but the gazed upon. Ichiro had taken the picture with one of his firm's remote-control cameras just before they came to Wales. 'Sachi, my dearest', he had written on it. That was what he called her in private. Now, in their new country, he used it in public instead of Sachiko, which seemed to her like something cast off by another against her will, or something surrendered reluctantly at Customs.

She collected her walking-boots, so tiny they made her grin, and placed them on the back seat of her car with the bobble-hat and the windcheater. The company had provided them with a big house on its own in the country. It was too big, really, but there was a lot of entertaining involved in being Mrs Kuroda. Ichiro had taken ages to choose. At each likely property, in similar locations to the one he had finally picked, he would race to the first upstairs window, then to the highest point in the garden if it weren't flat, and train his binoculars on the horizon. Only at their chosen site did he obtain a view of a green landscape unfolding tumultuously into purple-saddled hills and jagged spoil heaps. One wintry morning, not long after their arrival, Ichiro woke her and led her excitedly to the bedroom window, offering her the glasses. The tip above distant Pantmoel was snow-capped. 'Mount Fuji!' he cried.

Mrs Kuroda's Mazda showed the beginnings of rust at its hem. She drove it through the gates and let it roll down the slope, through the tunnel of trees. It had been another one of Ichiro's ideas for her to buy a secondhand car which would demonstrate that she was neither ostentatious nor concerned to present all things Japanese as faultless. 'In any case,' he had told her, 'this is the car of our people' – our people meaning the workers at his Pantmoel electronics factory. She went along with these harmless subterfuges. Ichiro's energy made her breathless. He was so sure of himself that she was swept along by his enthusiasm. She had the feeling of always being in his wake, but an affectionate smile over his shoulder every so often would reassure her. He knew all this; he was conscious of having to look back every time he craved her sweet, doll-like features. That was how the sinecure had come about. That was why he had placed her in charge of the Home Club, for the company's middle management and their families.

Tears were welling as she pulled up at the city junction ready to drive north to the Beacons, and they broke like dammed waters as she giggled at the small roadside hoarding. BILL POSTERS WILL BE PROSECUTED it said in bold multiples. Bill had explained the joke, which hadn't been all that difficult to understand with her good command of English, but she had not found it as funny as he had. It wasn't all so unproductive where she and Bill were concerned. He had begun by telling her about the past of Wales and the need to embrace a different Welsh future.

He'd told her that her face was like the dawn, on the afternoon he'd introduced her to the story of the ill-fated Gelert. She laughed again through her tears as she recalled her comical attempts at pronunciation. 'Smith-er-reens, Mab-in-og-ion,' she had repeated between her little high-pitched cries of glee. Ichiro had heard her practising the words in the kitchen.

'What's that, Sachi?' he had called from the doorway, lowering his opened newspaper to waist height.

'Oh nothing,' she had replied. 'More English sayings.'

Mrs Kuroda worked hard at her job. Turning up the valley parallel to the one where Ichiro was at that moment addressing his assembled workforce on the impending need for redundancies, she heard the Home Club documents on the back seat cascade to the floor like a column of slates. She didn't care. Her tears were as much for poor Dr Kagoshima, due to arrive from the Osaka plant at the weekend as for anyone else, including herself. Even Dr Kagoshima, coming with bad news from the East but due to be confronted with all that was positive in his Western empire, even the modest Pantmoel Home Club, could not take her far enough back. She remembered a scene from a film in which a teenage boy waited in vain for the return of the suicide pilots before clambering into the cockpit himself, white headband trailing, only for the engine to fail. It might have been old Dr Kagoshima. Both of them in their own ways had been born too late for the big events.

She pulled in at a lay-by which led down to the side of a small reservoir. It was where she and Bill had gone after the visit to the museum. 'My recent past,' he had called it. How thrilled she had been at the success of those first meetings.

Ideas and suggestions drifted against the Club's slender administrative structure, almost suffocating it with potential. In the dark evenings, she would sit at home under the standard lamp with her glasses balanced on the tip of her nose and map out the Club's course, while her husband, stretched out on the settee, examined the *Financial Times* in microscopic detail. She felt there was a sense in which he had found her something with which to occupy herself and was loath to intrude unduly.

One night, after a committee member had resigned through illness, she had written the name of William Posters in a vacant space in her minutes book. The surname was a deliberate mistake, and she had stifled a smile. She told her husband his real name. 'Do you know him, Ichiro?' she had asked, without looking up. 'No – oh, yes,' he had replied, and turned the page of his newspaper.

There were three ducks on the choppy waters, bobbing together against a stiff wind. A thousand wavelets broke together. Hers was the only car in the gravelled parking bay. She put on her hat and walked towards the water's edge, wrapping her arms around her to keep warm. For every wave a thought, collapsing to make room for another. The endless succession wearied her; the wind almost carried her away. She remembered giving Bill that first lift home after they had stayed late to discuss the Club's summer programme. It was he who had suggested the Japanese evening, the slide show, the tea ceremony. Then there was the time she had grabbed his arm as the cage plunged down the shaft at the museum. Then the phone calls to the Vale when Ichiro was at work, the vast silence of the house save for the wind chimes.

She looked up at the sloping main road high above the

reservoir and saw one of Ichiro's transporters, sleek in its blue and silver livery and catching the sun as it slid down from the hills towards the border with England. She could barely keep up with Ichiro's explanations of what was happening. She knew nothing could be done about his mother and her father, independently growing frail back home. Each time Dr Kagoshima came over, he reminded her with his hunched shoulders and thinning grey hair of the widow and widower, sitting silent in the groves of Wakamatsu.

Shivering as the wind rattled down from the Heads of the Valleys, she wondered what Ichiro would think of her acting independently beyond the space he had created. What would anyone think, come to that? On his first visit to the house, so long ago that its heart-thumping excitement had been transferred to thoughts of the future, their future, Bill had warned of the perils of being a woman alone in a remote house, describing a Wales in which all slept with their doors bolted at night, unlike the old days. She thought that her small stature made him over-protective. They certainly made an odd-looking pair: he big and brawny yet considerate and gentle of voice; she for ever on tip-toe, as if peering over a ridge, the better to catch sight of some forbidden territory. Perhaps it was out of bounds because Ichiro had already identified places which would remind her of home, sites of gaping dereliction with kids mimicking aeroplanes in flight, just like the black, water-filled 'bumps' of Nagasaki, where the aged saw their own ruination mirrored in the endless rubble.

She walked back to the car with her head bowed. Her tiny feet made scarcely a sound on the stones. Such lightness she felt now, as though she were disappearing into pure memory, out of range of all that might do her harm. She and Bill had exchanged old photographs of themselves at one of the Home Club's late sittings, while they waited for Ichiro to pick her up in his own car, hers having broken down impressively. The Japanese wives had changed into kimonos for the evening, and she recalled how, quick-stepping, they had fluttered colourfully across the play area of the leisure centre, where the Club's monthly-hired room made perfect neutral ground among the learners. In one of the pictures, Bill was a lively nine-year-old, straining forwards as a snow-haired great aunt held him in check for the photographer. Hers, too, were from an equally austere time. All was innocence then, in the days of struggle. As they shuffled the photos, passed them to each other and let them slip into a pile on the table between them, they took on the chaotic shape of destiny in the making. 'Little did they know,' she had thought, 'little did they know.'

While waiting to pull out on to the main road, she thought she spotted one of the wives – there were just five of them in the district – driving in the opposite direction. Her heart quivered like a momentarily trapped bird. But it was too late to be worried by ostracism. In fact, she wished something like that would happen, some trickle of evidence to release the pressure of all her piled-up pain and frustration. She even cursed the old car as it laboured up the slope towards the Beacons, its low gears groaning. Ichiro's success had not made the other wives particularly friendly. As appendages of their go-getting husbands, they were saturated with the influence of ambition, the prospect of once more moving on. This was not the engagement with Western ways she had yearned for as a girl; it was the old behaviour simply transferred to another place. In it she recognised the selfless but rough-shodden manner which, Bill said, had created so much ferment among the miners. He'd welcomed the arrival of Ichiro's factory but she knew when he had sighed so heavily at the museum's coalface – a huge black arrow-head, caught pincer-like by crushing stone above and below – that reality was one thing and dignity quite another. Now that his workmates all wore overalls with their names on, it seemed easier to dispense with their services. She imagined someone ripping off the old tags and sewing on new ones.

At the Storey Arms, she parked opposite the hostel and read Bill's letter again. He had handed it to her at the last Club meeting. (The old formality had been perishing beside her zeal for the new customs, so that even faint-heartedness could barely masquerade as shyness.) She ran her fingertips over the clear, steady handwriting. He had addressed her as 'Dear Sachiko'. She remembered how someone had described Bill as a 'gentleman'. What had that meant? Discretion, good manners, consideration for the feelings of others? In Nagasaki he would be considered a good match for someone like her. On the afternoon of his visit to the house, when Ichiro had phoned minutes earlier to say he had arrived safely in Doncaster for a meeting with Dr Kagoshima's team, she had almost crumbled under the weight of duplicity in a foreign land. Yet there had been a peculiar thrill attached to its shared nature, as though it were a rite of passage to a higher plane of happiness, some fresh and sanctioned departure in a new country. In Bill's embrace she might have been burying herself in the protective folds of the landscape he had commended to her with such pride of possession. She had lain on her bed in Nagasaki, reading of hills and valleys and a people moved instinctively to song. 'Dear Sachiko,' Bill's letter had said. 'We cannot go on. There is too much in the way.'

The long, worn path beckoned her to the summit. She closed her ears to the siren wind. How the other wives had giggled at the opera in Cardiff as Madama Butterfly tortured herself with ridiculous, old-fashioned feelings and Western music splashed everywhere like breakers on a strange but exciting shore. In the costly seats, sitting together with the others, the strangeness was not on stage but in her mind, reclothing the confusion of her thoughts.

She balanced nervously at the edge of the escarpment and gazed into the void. Her arms shot out. In the gardens of Wakamatsu the trees shivered and a wheelchair turned sharply on a polished floor.

Snow at Christmas

Before I can begin relating the events of December 26, 1988 (as far as personal recollection can be relied on), it will be necessary to say something about my cousin Gillian, who was adopted in 1976 at the age of five and was therefore seventeen on that strange Christmas weekend. Just before midnight on Christmas Eve it had begun to snow, gently at first, as if by stealth, and I felt privileged, as though I were the first to notice an unannounced change in the weather. There was no-one else about near the house we'd rented above St Ives Bay. All was dark and windless and a Christmas card winter was allowed to descend, like a stage curtain. I could be seen smoking one of Uncle Ted's festive cigars, a fuming silhouette in the kitchen door's rectangle of light, alone and marvelling.

Ted and Aunty Vera had been desperate for children before Gillian came along. Vera's infertility was almost an affront in a family whose women were renowned for shelling out kids almost annually. In the old days, of course, having issued a multitude, the mothers scarcely made it to fifty, except for those who rallied and carried on until they were in their late nineties, a hundred even. Gillian was a sweetie, with Shirley Temple hair and a ready laugh that often had her gasping for breath. Early on I began speculating on her origins. Aunty Vera and Uncle Ted, acting valiantly, sometimes had to shepherd her tantrums and bad behaviour under the umbrella of a cheekiness we all recognised. We were an abstemious family in which everyone had to make allowances, not least Gillian's parents.

My other four uncles and aunties were an impecunious lot, mostly as a result of their own devices, uppermost of which was a surly lack of ambition among the menfolk. They must have resented our exclusive holiday arrangements but not enough to place relationships at risk. They rarely went anywhere up to the late 1980s, when they discovered cheap holidays in Spain. In summer, our paths diverged. To this generalisation, Uncle Guy, the youngest, did not conform. He'd been in the navy and was still a bachelor. His behaviour was joyously spontaneous and his unmarried state appeared almost as much a slight as Aunty Vera's failure to conceive. But, unlike Vera, he was never in pursuit of a solution, though he was always on the move and therefore gave the appearance of searching for something. Now and again he turned up unannounced when we were away. To cynical family members he was 'a black sheep'.

It happened first in 1975, when we were renting a large villa on Corfu. It was also the first time our two families were under the same roof instead of having made side-by-side hotel bookings. Ted and Vera had begun the adoption process and were sometimes willing to talk about it, nervously I thought, sometimes not. It was very hot and we were plagued by mosquitoes. Vera's legs were peppered early on with bites, which she made worse by dabbing with a violet island remedy, making her lower extremities appear as though they had been stuck with flowers. We were having breakfast outside one morning when Guy just appeared in the road below as a bus pulled away. He stood there at first with his holdall, possibly unsure of what kind of reception awaited him, but then bounded up the path. We bellowed a greeting despite being slightly confused and incredulous. Of course, we were glad to see him. He had come overland from Marseille to catch the Brindisi ferry.

One of the poor uncles had been known to question Guy's sexuality, but only on the basis of his nine years as a sailor. Guy probably had a girl in every port, as they say. He knocked about with a mixed crowd at home, mainly from his various places of work, as he skipped from one job to another. There'd been rumours that he had made a girl pregnant but the accusing uncle thought this unlikely, the possibility of Guy's being gay (not a term we used then) over-riding the stigma of begetting on the body of a 'slut' an illegitimate child, for which accommodations could be made. 'Johnny, you old shagmaster – what's up?' These were Guy's first words to me that day, when we'd strolled down to the olive trees after lunch. We could hear the voices of the others in the distance, and the sounds of washing-up. I was just eight, with one brother and another to follow. Guy simply didn't care, or had let the word slip and couldn't be bothered to retrieve it.

Of all the members of our family, I found Gillian and Guy the most interesting – not the most loving or the most selfless or the most considerate; but with a dimension I couldn't figure out, an air of not so much mystery as fugitive and exclusive habitation that placed them for ever beyond us. I was already on the path that led towards them and away from the others. I knew the journey would have to be mine alone; they, if anything, would shift farther away, perhaps out of sight, denying me full knowledge. And timidity made reaching the destination even more difficult.

The fact is that my affinity with Gillian – I was ten when she landed among us – has always been reciprocated. She was a tomboy, and for some reason I preferred that to the unalloyed product of my two brothers. It was a sort of tease, an attempt to break into the male province, and therefore probably sexual, though I wasn't aware of that until she was older. Nor was Gillian herself. Once, in Beeches Wood, while we were playing hide-and-seek, she pressed herself inside a hollowed-out oak and deliberately kept her whereabouts concealed, well beyond what she must have known would be our annoyance and panic. The formal cry of 'Give up?' she suppressed, but whereas the others simply got bored and drifted off after she'd re-appeared, I gave her a friendly thump and put my arm around her, amazed that an act of cruelty could within seconds magnify a sense of relief and intimacy. Had that been deliberate? Vera used to say, a little fearfully, 'Our Gilly is very knowing.'. Guy was knowing too, in the sense of having, like Gillian, almost no detectable fondness for reflection. Ted used to say that Gillian just gets on with it. Guy also, I could have added.

When I was twenty and Gillian was fifteen, I fell in love with her. I knew such behaviour would be frowned upon or forbidden even though we weren't blood relatives. It wasn't really love on my part, just serious infatuation, and she must have viewed me as a convenient male anchorage while she figured out what the stirrings under her belt meant. She surprised me by knowing that too and joked about giving birth to a baby with webbed feet. Where did she get that kind of information? With others we went to the pictures a couple of times. We sat together. Once, I ran my fingers down her arm. She pouted, smiled and crossed her bare legs. Her arms were covered in golden down, which I found exciting. But it was not long before she had a boyfriend, one of many preceding that snowy Christmas in Cornwall. On her sixteenth birthday, she said something odd to me: 'You'll be there, won't you?' By ourselves for a moment in the kitchen, I gave her a present and kissed her, a peck, on the lips. Her eyes closed. After that she became a cousin again, a relative at arm's length, growing up as a much-loved family member. Between the age of five and ten, she'd holidayed with us a couple of times, along with Ted and Vera, our regular companions in travel. I was still excessively fond of her. But I had been almost to the brink. Whether she had or not, I never knew. I fantasised a lot, mainly about catching her if ever she fell. Being there, you see. Guy hadn't changed much, except for drinking more. Sometimes you smelled it on his breath. Gossip smouldered, flaring briefly now and then.

I can't remember who had suggested spending Christmas at Birch Cottage, St Ives. It was a cottage in name only and spread out on its half-acre in a dip between St Ives and Carbis Bay among clumps of exotic gunnera, which hovered with menace among the trees. Perhaps the others had got tired of Spain and we, mischievously, needed to go one step farther. Although available for holiday letting most of the year, the house had evidence in a downstairs storeroom of permanent residence; or perhaps its contents – among them two surfboards hanging from a cross-beam, roller skates, walking-boots, a toolbox, cobweb-covered oilskins on hooks – had been left by its last owners and the rental company hadn't got round to clearing the place. We turned up in two cars on Friday, December 23 at four o'clock. It was already dark, the town almost deserted. Cold rain was slanting in off the sea.

I often wonder if my mother and father were happy with three sons – me and Doug and Johnny – particularly as Gillian seemed to have been the making of Ted and Vera from the start. She gave them no cause to revise their innocent sense of wonder, which in adults is often a source of vulnerability. Innocence deflects curiosity, so that odd behaviour comes as a shock. I had a sense that Christmas in St Ives of being on the cusp of something, of knowing but not admitting that it would be the last time our two families would get together away from home. My father's moodiness had long worried my mother to the point of debilitation. Ted and Vera, having anguished over parenthood for so long, simply saw their anxiety take different forms as Gillian grew older, changed and attached herself to others, which they in particular must have read as the irretrievable loss of something hard won. None of these things stopped us enjoying ourselves. Some of us were just more philosophical about them. The rental people had provided an artificial Christmas tree with lights. We'd just finished piling presents around it when Ted offered me a cigar and I volunteered to make coffee, which was when I noticed the first snowflakes through the kitchen window. The kettle switched on, I lit the cigar, opened the back door and stared into the void.

After a minute or two, I heard a car slowly free-wheeling down the slope from the narrow top road and could see its one brake light going on and off. I somehow knew it was Guy, but even when he'd parked near the coastal path next to the house, taken his big seaman's duffel bag out of the boot and begun climbing the path towards me, I did not call the others, because for once I was not sure what sort of welcome he'd get. Things had changed. For instance, in obedience to some unspoken lurch in the way the world behaved, we still smoked but not in front of others if it could be avoided. As Guy came into the light and raised his head, the bag over his shoulder, I greeted him with a puff of smoke: 'Father Christmas, I presume'. He may have thought there was an edge to my voice, a lack of fulsome embrace, though my face had registered a genuine welcome. He just thumped me gently in the midriff and smiled, and I realised, if I hadn't before, that hierarchies, the self-conscious regulation of one's surroundings in order to deal with how people behave, were meaningless to him. In this non-threatening world, Guy and Gillian and others like them roamed. One could feel protective towards them if only their need for succour was even less keenly felt than their sense of danger, or was so because of their indifference.

Christmas day itself began with sunshine, the snow having fled Penwith's peninsular winds. Presents were exchanged. Guy's bag was topped with the ones he'd brought. We moved sluggishly towards lunch and afterwards we went for a walk along the coastal path. I smoked another of Ted's proffered cigars. We talked in ever-changing groups, until Gillian ended up with Guy and they walked for a long while together, twenty yards in front of the main group. Past the headland, we descended to Porthminster Beach. It was deserted, except for a gambolling and barking black dog, its owner out of sight. As usual there was barely any wave motion, the flat sea offering just a token breaker to the strand. There was a feeling of permanence about the scene, or an air of relief from human attention that some invisible force was wishing would last. The sand gave way reluctantly under our feet. We were interlopers. Though the sun was up, a lid of cloud was sliding in from the West, and the taste of the air was metallic, sickly marine. I wished we hadn't come.

On route up to town, Ted drew alongside me. 'Our Gillian,' he said. 'What do you think?' I imagined the inflections his query supported, concerning his adopted daughter's appearance, assumption of womanhood, outlook on life, ambition, fitness for dealing with fracture and tribulation. I also tried to imagine what parenthood must be like – the secrecy involved in all that solicitude for someone whose independence you willed. Then I wondered if he actually wanted to know what I thought of the couple still out ahead, specifically the match, for now Gillian had slipped her arm through Guy's and they were sharing a string of hilarious private exchanges, her head leaning against his shoulder. I told Ted I thought she was grown-up, and his head nodded with a score of rapid, smiling assents, meant to communicate that that was precisely the problem. I sensed that my answer had not been much help.

That night, Christmas night, we watched television. Only the parents were sober, offering us an unspoken and unsolicited lesson from the past. Austerity and privation – they'd known both and would never forget them. My gaze fell on Guy and Gillian, who were sitting side by side on the floor and leaning against a settee. Was I the only one to notice that Guy's arm was resting lazily on Gillian's breast?

Just before midnight they turned in, following the parents and leaving me, Doug and Johnny watching a documentary about the Beach Boys.

'This is the last time I do this,' Johnny said.

'Me too,' Doug said. 'It's ridiculous. All these bloody pensioners.' I thought they were referring to Brian, Dennis and company, just then harmonising in high register while crammed into a psychedelic sand buggy, a conjunction that made me laugh. My brothers looked towards me like a pair of Midwich cuckoos, clearly offended at what they mistakenly thought was a dismissal of their rebelliousness, exposed now by one drink too many.

Sleep wouldn't come. By two o' clock the house was silent except for someone snoring far away and the noises of an old building. I got up and looked through the window. There were flashes of white on the top road where the gulls were swooping past the streetlight like giant moths. The sky was starry, flickering in the cold. Then, the ceiling immediately above my south-facing window, the one looking out on to the sloping garden, brightened. A light had been turned on somewhere. I thought an animal might have tripped a security lamp so I waited for it to go out. But it stayed on. I got up again and put on my dressing-gown. Stepping on to the landing I was aware that the rest of the house was 'well away', as my mother called it. Footsteps, a light tread, wouldn't bother anyone. I stepped gingerly down the stairs, aware of the drop in temperature as I reached the hallway. At the far end of the south wing through an archway were the kitchen and the blister of a small conservatory. Opposite the kitchen was a study – locked – and the lumber room where the surfboards and oilskins were kept. But there was no longer any light, even if it had come from the house, inside or out. Making little or no noise, I switched on the kitchen light and took a biscuit from the cookie-jar, and then wandered down to the conservatory's sliding glass panels. As I passed the door to the lumber room I heard a faint clacking noise. I stopped. I don't know why, but I imagined it to have come from the two surf boards I knew were hanging from the ceiling. The door was slightly ajar. It was only then that I thought of intruders. Cornwall for us had long been the place where people had no need to lock up their homes at night, or so some old polo-necked 'salt' had once told us, when we were tousle-haired, pink and peeling. In an act I knew straightaway to have been silly, I hesitated then gave an almost inaudible knock. I pushed the door open.

In the downstairs light, the natural light the eyes get used to, I could see Gillian standing alone, naked. I recall every detail of that moment: the surfboards almost imperceptibly swaying, the absence of anyone else, the dark inverted triangle between Gillian's legs like something brazenly painted on, the expressionless face minutely transforming itself into the faintest of smiles, the bee-stung lips smeared with red gloss, the upturned forefinger moving to rest against lips mimicking a 'Shh' sound; but above all I remember the intense blue cold of that room and its abandoned contents, its lingering seaweed smell. The cold that is the sister of loneliness. I said nothing. I thought of an apparition, a dream, and quickly retraced my steps.

Lying in bed later, I realised that Guy must have crept out when I was in the kitchen and that Gillian hadn't managed to leave before I began wandering towards the conservatory. I must have imagined the smile. There cannot have been a smile. In just over twenty-four hours, we would be leaving that place, once Boxing Day had been spent in more drinking, eating and walking – and chatting about everything and everyone except ourselves. Guy and Gillian were even more outrageous, at one point paddling in the wilder waters of Porthmeor beach. I could sense the others looking at me, as if I were able, as the oldest of the wild generation, to censure or explain. Only my mother said anything. 'What's happening?' she asked, tugging at my sleeve on the path back to the cottage. 'I think you know what I mean.' I told her what I felt about Gillian and Guy. She shook her head in disbelief and pulled me closer.

Doug had been right. That lingering family fraternity had gone on for too long. Was it about not letting go, an unspoken belief in safety in numbers begun long before when poverty pressed people into communities, perhaps against their better judgement or natural inclination? Or did it all start with the desperately childless Ted and Vera, and then, when Gillian came along, our groping attempts to reach outside ourselves towards this threat to our impregnability?

That St Ives Christmas was twelve years ago. I haven't even been to Cornwall since. The place has become, during my absence and in my mind, its former self: primitive and struggling, in the manner of its salt-soaked forebears, who trudged streets reeking of fish oil. When I speak to Gillian now we joke about that Christmas at Birch Cottage, when I and everyone else seemed to be so concerned that she and Guy, 'two on their own' as my mother would have said, were beginning some vague dance of destruction.

For the joke was on me. If there was a louring atmosphere in that cottage it was because everyone was concerned for me and my own unconscious form of oddity. It all makes sense now. When Ted asked me on the first walk what I thought of Gillian, he wasn't concerned about her but about me, his solicitude even avoiding any reservation he may have had about his stepdaughter and me being a pair; and when my mother, on that final pull up from the beach, asked me what was happening, she was not referring to anything beyond what she thought was my own well-being.

It's just been a long resolution or, for most of the time, no resolution at all. I was never much aware of anything inside forcing an issue. Perhaps I was too anxious for outcomes in others. Only once have Gillian and I talked about that incident, or whatever it was, in the lumber room. She said she'd fallen, and that I was there, as promised. I didn't let on, but the smile that crossed her lips was the very same I'd witnessed that night as she stood in the freezing cold, in her own world, the embracing repository of my love but forever untouchable. Guy's name, like its possessor gone roaming in places undiscovered, was not mentioned. Poor Guy – once thought by his actions to have been like me, whose inaction and steadfastness, inherited from my once impoverished parents, delayed the moment when I would turn up not so much unannounced as with a shocking announcement to make.

Ornithology

It's the migration I cannot bear, the going away, the estrangement posing as its opposite, the one I love being exactly that – 'one', 'her', 'she'. I must have picked it up from the doctors, who minister to third persons, the nameless, so that they don't get involved. But I am so, so involved with her, though she is now set apart. It, the unspoken, has stepped between us. Like is repelling like. She truly moves in mysterious ways and I, the godless, pray for her return. I want her back, to be reunited with her self. First name, surname; genus, species.

What is it they say – you only fully appreciate the little things of life when they are gone? How useless other ways of uttering these obvious truths sometimes seem. Especially when a struggle is involved to restore their depth; you always feel that the effort obscures the truth and isn't really worth the bother.

I was considering all this the evening I looked up at the first of the year's housemartins, which were flickering below the eaves like the ignition of a tiny straw fire. They arrive each year almost to the day – first the daring outriders, then the rest, wreathing the house with invisible garlands. Apart, that is, from two years before, when only a couple of them turned up, investigated the old nests and flew somewhere else. It was just after the lapwings failed to show in the field opposite.

'I miss their madness in the air,' she said. (I'd like to add 'prophetically', but truth's strangeness bars me.)

'Their flocks have been decimated. Perhaps the same has happened to the housemartins, some far-off, cosmic grab at bird life that has left its remnants to perform without support or not at all.' Everything I began saying to her sounded like something lifted from a book. It was as if intimacy would invite trouble.

That summer without housemartins enabled me to climb a ladder and hammer their abandoned nests to dust.

'Be careful,' she said, with a hint of reproof.

Standing below, she almost got showered in the stuff. Her arms were folded in the manner that denotes impatience, especially in women, in mothers waiting for a naughty child to admit its wrongdoing. They remained folded even when she stepped aside to avoid the crashing fragments, toeing back on to the concrete path a piece that had fallen on the lawn. What I didn't understand was how strongly the non-appearance of the birds affected her.

I knew, of course, that it had; such events, the lacunae created in routines and natural cycles, had long begun to leave her silent, first for hours, then for days. She'd always been what others call 'quiet', which for the uncharitable meant not awkward, not a bother. The only compensation for such people was a sense of humour, but in those like her its backswing of cruelty limited deployment.

'I always feel the bump whenever someone slips on a banana skin,' she said once, at a party. Everyone laughed except her. She looked down and tried to submerge the cherry in her cocktail with an outstretched finger, its nail chewed to the quick.

At the start, it was something that attracted me to her. It enabled me to see in her an aspect of myself that, unexpressed, allowed it to flower without being wounded by comparisons.

You can read any number of books on depression and be no closer to understanding it. I pick them up in bundles and go through them when she is away for a long time. But concentration is difficult. I am for ever thinking back to what people did before problems like hers were even recognised. Then I am distracted by what is going on around me, with the curious result that I come to resemble the impatient onlookers of yesteryear, who must have been irritated at least by an individual's retreat from joy and responsibility. I feel like that sometimes, as if I were the injured party and she is not so much withdrawing into herself as shrinking from my irksome presence. Perhaps I am partly to blame for the way she is. Who knows? I do know I'd be accused of saying these things while she was unable not so much to defend herself – what was to defend? – as have her say. Except that she has been saying very little. Perhaps I am speaking up for her against the 'pull yourself together' school of reparation.

Then, of course, there are the little red books.

Early in our marriage and before either of us could see the gathering clouds, she began keeping a diary. She announced her intention quite openly. We were shopping one day when she entered Woolco's and bought a wad of notebooks. Her first entries might almost be joint efforts, since they are about things she and I did together that required no discussion or afterthought. Then she writes comments on books she has read, films we have seen, Bresson's *Au Hasard Balthazar*, for instance: *At the end, at night, the donkey lies down among a flock of sheep but we do not know that it has been shot accidentally by a hunter. I knew. I knew by then, through men's cruelty, that it had earned its sanctity, that it was a symbol of saintliness, before B told me.* I remember telling her. 'Telling' may have been sarcastic.

Our garden was evidently planted by a previous occupant who ensured that somewhere there would be colour at all times – yellow jasmine in winter and fiery berries in autumn, as well as the overture and chorus of colours in spring and summer, and these appearances are noted for future reference. So exposed are her jottings that she always leaves the books lying around with a biro marking the page she is on. I think the books are symptomatic of what is waiting to ambush her and her need to keep intact something already under unannounced threat. Diarists who do not succumb never realise how much they contribute to their continuing integrity by daily lowering their noses to the page and scribbling away.

Just after I knocked down the housemartins' nests – I could never do it properly because there is always a horseshoe of muck left where the first frantic adhesions are made – she suffered her worst spell. I always have to guess how she is interpreting an event that to me is an extension of experience, like the lumps of clay the housemartins use to build up their miraculous orbs. I found her in the kitchen, her arms still folded, waiting for me to admit a wrong I was unaware of and reminding me of a child which finds itself taking the blame for someone else's misdemeanour. Within hours, she had gone upstairs and cut herself.

Even though I am alert to unusually long silences following her disappearance from my sight – I cannot just trail her – I missed the event itself. Calling her without reply, I pushed open the bathroom door and there she was, sitting side-saddle on the edge of the bath, bleeding from a wrist wound and looking up at me, her head inclined, with a sort of religious pity. Her damaged arm was resting upturned on her knee, and the blood – not much of it, to be sure – was running down her leg. I noticed that several tears had dripped on to it, clearing a purified channel for themselves. Seduction by inessentials.

'Look', she said, pitifully.

It was as if the harm done was somehow wondrous, external to herself.

'For God's sake,' I enjoined. 'What have you done?'

She stared at me curiously, as a child falsely accused stares at a denouncing adult.

Days later, on my return from the hospital and for the first time, I opened one of the red books.

I use the word 'diary', but there are no dates. I recognised an analysis of a strange foreign film we went to, not like Bresson's, but one of those avant-garde movies composed of seemingly unrelated events and images, though some things, possibly motifs, kept repeating themselves, as if the director had been saying to the audience, those bemused phantoms in the half-light: 'Come on – can't you see what I'm getting at?' We laughed off our incomprehension at the time, but the book records no amusement. There is a description of rooks' nests 'snagged' in the treetops. Poetic, I think. Then there is a reference to 'R', who has come to tick her off about something. I look at the other books. 'R' makes regular appearances. Fairly soon, the identity of 'R' becomes my obsession. Woman's malady, old flame, spectre, the spreading ink blot of melancholy, alter ego, friend from the past, substitute confessor – whoever it is, the visits are frequent, their reasons ambiguous: 'R' will understand, 'R' will sort it out, 'R' would never have approved. On one page 'R' is reprimanded for reneging on a promise, on another thanked for turning up (*It was great to see you*). I feel the enlivening rush of jealousy, that curious repositioning it causes when you suddenly see a loved one in a different light and begin courting its relative, gnawing speculation.

So partly as an attempt to join her in whatever world she is describing in the books, I start to look upon 'R' as a real person – 'Robbie' – not some ghostly companion she's invented. In her moments of release, as the doctors call them, she is as lucid as anyone else and as capable as I of subterfuge and duplicity. We often talk about whether we are ever likely to strike up another relationship and vow to be open about it. But we both know it probably won't happen that way, because an 'affair' – a word that tickles us both – is clandestine almost by definition, something that denotes a temporary state, full of truth and expectation at the same time but just about holding its self-destructive tendency in check. Anyway, we never open each other's mail, not even when it's a bank statement or a flyer for car insurance. There are always letters for each of us whose

137

contents the other cannot divine. When she's 'away', her mail piles up. But the novelty of identification soon wears off. I imagine Robbie finally waving farewell with a smile – not the smile of a fugitive's triumph but one of the simpering sort that marks the passing of a trite, insubstantial character. Maybe it went with her to the hospital below Holy Mountain.

She will get to the phone at all hours and say: 'It's me.'

Irritating. Who do I think it is? Once, I heard a scream in the background, some other's torment. 'Are you all right?' I asked. 'Is anything the matter?' In the silence that followed, I was invited to ponder my awkwardness: 'I mean, has anything happened?'

There are plans to accommodate spouses and other carers in the grounds, to minimise travel. One morning, before visiting, I gained the summit, domain of buzzards, to see the place from a distance, a height. Apart from a Victorian façade, the buildings are fairly new but remind me of the Maze Prison, with their image of capital letters stamped into the ground. Make a name, I muttered, make a name. It was spring, and a few skylarks spun out of the heather at my approach. The way down was rocky and painful, unlike the ascent.

At home the calls from friends and family are less frequent, but there is little to report, except to say that she is still battling. Doing so reminds me of issuing bulletins on someone who has decided to explore the Amazon alone: either they'd succumb or they wouldn't and from the beginning they are always making for home. It is a case of awaiting their return, should Providence will it.

But I suppose it seems heartless to talk about anything else at length. I imagine the countless things people do or care about, some of which they forget. It is not a question of priorities, it is that everything is a priority. At any moment, one of them might be nursing a recurrent pain, or become mystified at a daughter's strange behaviour, or notice that of late the boss seems always to be questioning their judgement. As long as she is in capable hands, that's all that can matter to them.

But I still cannot get out of my mind that she is forgotten until someone decides to make inquiries about her. I even forget her myself. The year after the housemartins' non-appearance, I saw a swallow on a telephone wire, its forked tail unmistakeable. It was early for returning migrants but patterns were changing. Still, I couldn't help thinking I'd been a sole witness to something, and for a while, totally absorbed, I watched for others to begin circling the old barn that stood on my neighbour's property. I hoped the housemartins wouldn't be far behind. It would be something positive to tell her.

I went out the next evening to wait after replacing her notebooks where she had left them. The sun, still high in the west, seemed reluctant to set. I'd read somewhere that birdsong was a fraction of what it used to be. The coming of the silent spring. So what I heard was a stragglers' chorus. I tried to imagine how some people could not come to terms with such knowledge. I spend a lot of time just standing in the garden, pondering.

I looked up at the housemartins' imprints from the previous summer and whispered to myself: 'Is it me? Could it be me?' And I waited for a flicker, a sound – some sign before nightfall outside the empty house of a bird trailing a name.

Cherry Hill

The weather-worn ruins of the old town of Les Baux rise to a cliff's edge, from which medieval noblemen pushed malcontents to their deaths as a deterrent. Even today, the fertile plain rolling away from the foot of the cliff is an antidote to the evidence of the town's last remaining function as a lazaretto. With their backs to despair, the victims of executioners, vain or insidious, must have contemplated a future paradise. For this much at the very least, I am indebted to a pair of dogged expatriates, Bee Compton and Mavis Smith. It was among the ruins that I first came across Bee's shadow, approaching mine like an oil slick over the bleached stones.

'You are a sad woman, very sad,' she said.

I turned to discover the thinnest person I had ever seen. She could scarcely stand in the wind, which had sped across the flatlands from Arles and was dispersing wildly on the cliff top. In her white dress with the blue polka dots she might have taken off, like a kite. I would normally have walked away from the sound of an English voice in France, especially the hectoring sort with its air of tired familiarity aimed at children; but hers was different, almost solicitous.

'Would you help me?' she inquired. 'I find pilgrimages so arduous. Necessary, but arduous.' She held my arm. 'Not the religious sort. I mean journeys to the countries of the heart.'

She was staying in a small house in the valley, her 'command HQ'. From the cliff could be seen three other *villages perchés* in different directions; they crowned hills which rose from the quilted valley bottom on shoulders of hot, white rock. We stepped on to a circular viewing-platform and it was as if we were suddenly spinning through the molten white sky of a Provencal noon. Once the reason for my condition, my sadness, had been established intuitively, she lost interest, staring instead at a figure approaching from the direction of the cemetery. This was Mavis, coming at us with a shuffling hesitation. They could almost have been twins.

It was a relief to be free of the vast tourist drift. By definition, Tim was always in my thoughts. I saw his death as my loss only, unconnected with how his brothers and parents felt. It had no purifying effect. It made me even more selfish than normal. Into the void it left poured all manner of experience, especially that proscribed by a happy marriage. The outward flow of emotion, so supporting and protective, had reversed its course to become unfamiliar but exciting.

We seated ourselves on the terrace of a café and Bee began telling me what she thought of France and the French. 'Take churches, my dear,' she said. 'Dingy places on the whole, badly lit by a tight-fisted clergy and full of awful paintings.'

'Great in hot weather, though,' Mavis chipped in. 'You can't beat sitting astride a damp sarcophagus when you're feeling sticky and the vicar is out of sight.'

'*Curé*, dear,' Bee said. 'You'll get us bloody well shot one day.'

'Pay no attention,' Mavis advised. 'In my book, discretion and valour are coterminous.'

They seemed to have arrived at some kind of mutually agreed antipathy, not just on this question of decorum but possibly on other matters as well. They glanced about at the other customers, as if for confirmation of their views. In their dark glasses they resembled long-forgotten celebrities hoping for recognition among peers.

'So what's up, dearie?' Bee asked.

I told them. They stared at me as though I were an adolescent confessing to a raffish priest.

'Yes, well, we've all gone through it, haven't we Mave?'

'Oh yes,' Mavis said. 'We've done the mourning bit.' She examined me closely. 'But you're too young to be a widow.'

'Was he handsome?' Bee asked, cutting her short.

I'd never thought of Tim as handsome. I supposed he was.

Mavis allowed her arms to dangle beside her chair. I think she was bored with these revelations. 'So what do you think of Les Baux?'

'Impressive,' I said.

'You wouldn't think that if you had to struggle up here every morning for bread,' Bee answered. 'Not that we have to. We usually send Bertie – for the exercise.' They chuckled.

'Probably takes it out of him,' Mavis said, hypnotised by the deft movements of the waiters. 'And the tourists are something awful, present company excluded.' She turned to me with her elbows planted on the table. 'Did you know that the Romans trained dogs to chase old mules off the cliff as a form of entertainment?' She registered shock, as if the fact still made her incredulous. 'I mean, can the practice of slave-holding be mitigated by the achievements of a so-called civilisation? Indeed, is the expression "slave-holding civilisation" a contradiction in terms?'

Bee nodded as these questions were put, not so much at their relevance, more at their rhetorical weight. The single-mindedness that attracted one to the other, like opposite poles, had been transformed into an almost aggressive consensus. Bee had only to smile at me as her companion spoke to convince me of this. They had left the familiar behind and were on a two-woman journey of discovery. I was going through the same experience alone. One incident in particular illustrated this: in a darkened hotel room at Le Puy, Tim had made love to me all afternoon, perhaps atoning for something we lacked in the routine procedures of the night. The sort of skirmishing which made all-out war inevitable had begun.

Bee and Mavis escorted me to the courtyard in front of the little church. In the valley were clusters of flat-roofed homes, some with swimming pools and clay tennis courts, spliced by the flaming cypresses of Van Gogh. Bee pointed out the place where she and Mavis were staying with Bertie. There was an old car in the drive. I stared at the scene but was not concentrating; I couldn't get Tim out of my mind. I felt that I was working him out of my system and that the process, hastened somehow by meeting these two odd women, was nearing its end. Was I still grieving?

A month after Tim's death, I read a book on how to cope

with grief. I accepted that it reduced you to a helpless state in which any kind of assistance was always available if not welcome. This was what was meant by death's being a leveller. I suppose that my journey was a descent in more ways than one and that what so many hated or feared about death was its exposure of a self-reliance built on the shaky stilts of an education. The book set deadlines for recovery and renewal. It was too facile. For a long time, I felt deserted. Tim, gone from me, became the focus of my resentment.

'You shouldn't dwell on things,' Mavis said.

'Dwell?'

'Don't deny it,' Bee said. 'Geography revisited is but the skeleton of a lived-through joy.' (I had let slip that all the places on my itinerary were those I'd visited with Tim.)

'Would you like to see where they landed?' Mavis asked me.

I looked puzzled.

'The donkeys and, for that matter, the rebels. Apparently, that was a spectacle and a half, *aussi*. I suppose that if you're at a fairly safe distance there's little to choose in terms of your own sensitivity between the suffering of Roman animals and the wretchedness of fifteenth-century humans. What do you say?'

'I'd love to see it.'

'Didn't mean that, silly!'

We walked the short distance to the foot of the cliffs, with Bee and Mavis leading like a pair of tourist guides. The wind had dropped to a warm breeze. It must have been there, on that downward path, that Cocteau had filmed scenes from *Le Testament d'Orphée*. I looked straight in front, over and beyond the heads of the two women, towards the flat, livid fastnesses of Provence. Huge distances, their detail lost in the haze, spoke of eternity: now comforting, now unsettling. A hundred years before, Dumas and Merimée had visited Les Baux to find only a handful of beggars living there, confused I suppose by the same prospects of hope and damnation.

'Just along here,' Mavis said, negotiating a huge boulder.

'We found out about the games,' Bee said. 'You've got to in this country. Some places are obsessed with labelling the past. Here, they seem to live it.' I knew what she meant. I'd stopped off at Chartres: at the end of the day I'd half expected to hear the slapping sandals of a gang of cowled lay brothers come to sluice down the nave.

Mavis and Bee strolled about while I leant against another large rock. It was a sheer drop from the precipice directly above. Suddenly, Mavis shouted: 'Yoo-hoo!' She was looking up at a tiny silhouette, which first offered a timid wave then began flapping its arms in imitation of a birdman.

'It's Bertic,' Bee explained.

For an instant, he was not Bertie at all but the representative of some other, faraway region, dimly acknowledging the gulf between us. I remembered that it was something Tim often did, forging ahead to make the discovery about a new place, whatever it was, and beckoning me forward – calling my name out loud as if I were a child. I don't mean to be unkind when I recall that Tim possessed little imagination. It's just that the differences between couples which early on are submerged by desire ultimately become the sources of hostility. I guess that this was an imaginative assessment on my part of the state of our relationship. When I look back on that afternoon in the bedroom at Le Puy it is always with the feeling that Tim's lack of perception had prevented him from recognising a more vital self exposed by new conditions. If I smiled as he moved above me it was because I formed this idea of a miracle happening in a place which thrived on a solemn and eternally-deferred hope of the miraculous. I remembered saying as he bore down on me yet again that the wooden Virgin on the wall was shedding tears, but in his ecstasy he must have mistaken my laughter for a distant expression of pleasure, which was never reconstructed with the same intensity. Foreign ways for foreign parts.

Later, as I faced Bee and Bertie across the veranda table of their house on the Arles road, it occurred to me that they had packed away these kinds of thoughts for good. Where Bee and Mavis were concerned, lengthy introductions seemed unnecessary. Bertie's relationship to them was more obscure. As a wanderer moving idly from one point of remembrance to another, I had simply latched on to them because they offered no resistance. I had nothing else to do, save draw close to new worlds. I walked down from Les Baux on the cusp of the little crescent they formed by linking arms. I wondered whether people who had come to terms with worry ever wished it had happened earlier.

Bee was at the back of the house, pouring lemonade into tall glasses. She caught my eye. 'Help with these, dearie, would you?'

The inside was almost bare: a few sticks of furniture appearing to hold down a worn central carpet of vaguely Moorish pattern. Yet this impression of temporary residence was itself tacked into place by framed photographs of airmen in leather combat jackets. Some were posed like cricket teams in front of Spitfires and other aeroplanes, each a monster poking its eager snout skywards; others were of the same man with the same square jaw, broad smile and wavy blonde hair. All the photos were gathered about a mounted shield crowned by a set of wings. It reminded me of a shrine, a collection of portable icons, which I guessed was what it was.

'I should get some sort of bally medal for it,' Bertie said as he supped his drink. 'The French might keep their kiddy-winkies on a lead but that doesn't go for the rest.' It appeared that an Arab toddler had wandered too close to the cliff edge; he had grabbed her just in time and returned her to her ungrateful guardians. 'I don't know why there isn't a Danger sign up there.'

Mavis sighed. 'If you'd only keep your eyes open you'd know that a country like France is all past. Its present is trivial and its future is sinister or ugly or a combination of both.' Bee concurred. The return of the theme in Bertie's presence made it seem as if they had rehearsed it especially for his benefit.

'Bertie wants everywhere to be like the old country, only better,' Bee said. 'Restrictions all over the place so that we would all have something to complain about.'

'Poor old Bertie,' Mavis observed. 'Every gallant act undercut by stupidity.'

Bertie smiled across as if inviting me to accept that his cheerfulness would remain invincible no matter how smartly it was chafed by a brighter intellect.

'Personally, I think the world has seen worse things than poor knaves made to step into oblivion,' he said. 'After all, this country has a record of making a drama out of an execution.'

'You are mistaking the plebs for the patricians and a gruesome pastime for a necessary act,' Mavis argued. 'Even in countries with capital punishment the claim to decency is that they don't actually enjoy it. It's not a party.'

'Anyway,' Bee added, 'we're talking about consequences, never mind the road-building and the pretensions to steward-ship. The goings-on up there are reminders of a certain grotesque mentality.' Her wizened features proclaimed that this was a statement hard won by herself and her ilk. Mavis, of course, nodded agreement.

I felt sorry for Bertie and was relieved when Bee asked if I would like to join them for a dip in the pool. Bertie declined to join us. 'It's a good job he was grounded,' said Mavis, cryptically. 'Sod's Law would have brought him down in the drink, and no mistake.'

As I rested on my elbows at the shallow end of the pool, Bee and Mavis paddled towards me on either flank, their bathing caps like tinselled chocolate Easter eggs. For a moment I had the odd sensation that they were being propelled by motors but this turned out to be a microlight plane which must have passed overhead regularly for all the notice the three took of it. Their indifference made me think of some shared physical defect, such as blindness or deafness, or both of these. I wondered if I had imagined it. I looked up and saw that Bertie had lit a cigar and was releasing his first mouthful of smoke. As the plane cast its shadow the smoke obliterated his face. 'Put me out,' he seemed to be saying, 'I'm on fire!' The women touched the end of the pool together with their long red fingernails.

'Stay the night,' Bee suggested.

'Yes, do,' Mavis said. 'We'll bring you breakfast.'

Bertie just sat there, paralysed by some private reverie. He seemed to know his place. I, too, was dreaming – about that final chapter in which I was to be left on my own, a widow.

For all his faults, I would love to have seen Tim jewelled by water like Bee and Mavis were, as though mortality stumbled forever in his wake. When his biopsy results came through and we were both asked to report to the health centre together, the well-meant ineptitude of the summons made us chuckle. Laughter then was a major event. We had braced ourselves for the worst, and the unofficial tidings made us feel as sorry for Mrs Hopkins, the centre's receptionist, as we did for each other. I remember the drive there: rigid with foreboding, I thought about Mrs Hopkins and her continual arrival at grim knowledge through form-filling, card-indexing and the faint marks of bureaucracy. She waved us through in silence. I also remember Tim's profile, slowly declining away from me towards the surgery window. Six months, a year if we were lucky. It turned out to be eight months of warfare against an implacable enemy, and it was a lingering death.

I think Bee was the first to begin talking of Cherry Hill, the Second World War airfield in East Sussex. As she described the place – an expanse with hangars like giant woodlice and Spitfire pilots relaxing, waiting, in the sun on battered settees – it merged into a picture from every film I'd ever seen about the Battle of Britain. But it could have been Mavis or even Bertie who told me, though almost everything Bertie said was either contradicted or ridiculed, and this made him an early faller in the race to impart wisdom and recollection. We drank a lot. All I retain is a vague picture of a deserted, moonlit airfield near Lewes. Then again, the scene might have been up in the old town, where I dreamt we'd walked to. There was laughter from other parts of the house after I turned in, a sort of mischievous laughter. I thought of how tamely Bee and Mavis struggled to construct separate personalities for themselves. They were all confident talk. I cannot remember whether the two had each loved the airman – dead in battle, of course, leaning at full tilt on a Messerschmitt, teeth bared – or whether I had supplied this information fancifully to myself. Bertie was, or could have been, the pilot's brother; it made sense, the image of a pleasant-enough duffer in a hero's sloughed skin, saved from the ignominy of a belly-flopper in the Channel to live on, blazered and benign, among determined women of indeterminate rank. He was in league with them, the laughter told me, he was their disciple. I can see him now, standing on the topmost rampart, keeping watch as Bee and Mavis pick their way towards me with their arms stretched before them and their palms upturned. Over the rattling stones they come on that final walk to the spot beyond which the dead flash in their courses like shooting stars. Did I dream, too, that this was my punishment for not knowing that to die young is to be deprived of a life which the survivor must seek to redeem?

I packed up early next morning before breakfast and left a note. Through a chink in the door to one of the bedrooms I could make out the cathedral effigies of Bee and Mavis. In another room, Bertie was sleeping unclothed.

My destination was Clermont-Ferrand, but first I had to

make for Thiers, then travel a little farther south to the campsite at Escoutoux. Butterflies were thick among the asphodels. It had been the same when Tim and I had spent the night there and I discovered him sunbathing the next morning with three Swallowtails drinking at the stream of sweat running down the middle of his chest. I'd taken a photo of it, but had forgotten to bring it with me on that final outward journey of remembering. I positioned my forgetfulness alongside the relentless remembrance of Bee and Mavis and wondered if I was at all like them. At all like Tim, for that matter. From my window seat on the fast train home, the countryside rushed by, but I will always remember it as drifting slowly, into the past.

Coker's Mule

My Uncle Ben always exaggerated, which meant he was often lord of a vacant annexe, but I believed him when he told me that the Italian prisoners-of-war had been trusted to work in the fields near Coker's Wood. It seemed inconceivable that their regime of inspired lassitude could have been overridden by a patriotic urge to escape.

I recall being taken to the compound ten years after the war, when I was thirteen. The huts were still standing, but the high fence had been removed and the silver birches planted by the prisoners as saplings inside it were already forming an expanded arbour. They softened the memory of confinement and in a strange way were a comment on it, as though salvation could emerge from oppression in almost the same image.

Coker's Wood rose in a westerly direction, and beyond it was the farm itself. It was to this place on warm summer mornings and snow-draped winter ones that Uncle Ben and his fellow guards would escort their charges for agricultural duties, to which Bruno and the others brought a gritty

Tuscan efficiency. They mucked out stables and repaired fences; they helped break in horses and dipped sheep. So sure was old man Coker of their character that he allowed them to help with the killing of chickens and geese at Christmas, with knives made thin and lethal by much use. (It was Coker, a cynical, sloping figure, who likened Uncle Ben's responsibilities to the cosseting of lambs and suggested that Bruno and his friends knew they were on to a good thing.)

When recounting all this, Uncle Ben would fix me with a steady gaze. At eight every morning, on rising, he would clamp a pipe between his teeth, light it with a fuss of sucking and biting, and not remove it permanently until late in the day. His eyes watered, irrigating the furrows of his skin, so that he appeared to be in a state of perpetual lament. He had remained a bachelor and had survived without a reputation for womanising – unusual in that frisky region down from the hills – but at thirteen I found it hard to reconcile the ruddy cherubic status this conferred on him among the virtuous with his watery, mesmerising scowl. At that age I felt he was wondering whether or not I had yet plundered the only secret that really mattered and one to which he claimed sole dominion. But Uncle Ben's dominions tended to be shaky.

He rose from his chair one Saturday morning, as I was struggling with one of his boiled sweets, and pulled a folder from a drawer.

'See this?' he mumbled. 'Bruno did it.'

It was a sheet of paper on which horses in various positions had been sketched with a pencil. In a corner was written, 'To Sergeant Beniamino from Bruno Siepi!' A talent for art ran in one side of my family and there were pictures on the wall at home. One of Bruno's drawings showed a colt rolling in the grass, its flattened belly like a sack of corn and its vicious legs kicking out, celebrating release. Uncle Ben was fond of reminding me that I had not inherited any artistic skill, and my attempts to copy Bruno's efforts made him laugh.

A few years later, Sunday tea at Uncle Ben's house in the village became a tired ritual. I was off to university and was already overbearing. My parents had long ceased to accompany me. Though always dutiful, I'd rapidly grown tall and boorish. One day, while we had our heads under the bonnet of his Ford Anglia, Uncle Ben told me of a plan to clear the compound and build a row of council houses.

'A good thing,' I said provocatively. 'It just offers an excuse for old warriors like you to play the storyteller.'

'Rubbish!'

I knew he couldn't defend himself. It was the wrong time. The Festival of Britain had come and gone. A monstrous gear was grinding throughout the land. I was to study philosophy while my father's generation was firing more and more rivets into more and more washing machines.

'You know what they say: step out of a river and step back in again and it's a different river, totally different.'

Tobacco ash dropped on to his arm. I wondered why he had never married. I saw the pipe as a talisman protecting him against the advances of women. I imagined two people arriving at sex so late that they had to make do with its embers without having experienced its wildfire. I had come to believe that those who expected little deserved less.

'In any case,' I said. 'You didn't really like those Eyeties.'

'Bastards!'

'Except Bruno.'

'Bruno was all right.'

He had a habit, like my father, of only answering certain questions and making the others sound rhetorical through silence. His lack of response indicated that he'd obviously thought about this himself.

'Let's try again and then I'll show you something,' he said.

I flopped into the driver's seat, held the choke out and turned the ignition. After two spasms and a lot of whining the engine started. Uncle Ben appeared from behind the bonnet, re-lighting his pipe. Without looking at me but positioning himself so that I could see him, he made signs for me to push the choke in gently. He wouldn't tell me what had gone wrong: it might have taken too much away from the triumph of common sense over intellect, then as now a dirty word. He once expressed doubts about a philosopher's ability to raise a stranded car from a ditch, given a fixed number of seemingly unrelated tools. I must have responded with some superior-sounding remark about what kind of philosopher.

Uncle Ben illustrated the fact that if children enjoy a stable relationship with their parents they will discover more interesting forms of vitality only in ever-increasing circles away from the core of their happiness. Once I had returned the love of my mother and father, nothing else about them seemed worth noting. At the time I did not feel that this was callous. Through them I came to appreciate the idea of an almost unsullied goodness and how few lived up to it, hard though they tried. Perhaps this was why tragedy always struck at families and why aunts and uncles and the eccentric legions of relatives beyond them were always good for a laugh, notwithstanding that each one was the centre of something or other.

Although I knew the countryside around Uncle Ben's place, I had no idea where he was taking me. In any case, the journey was punctuated by leaps and hops as the car started playing up again. Uncle Ben was slapping the steering wheel and looking straight ahead, determined to avoid ignominy. After another minute of being rocked about, the ride became smoother and Uncle Ben's pipe rose slowly in the corner of his mouth as part of the mechanism of grinning.

Soon, I realised we were heading for Coker's Farm, because the fork in the road we'd taken near the reservoir led unsuspecting walkers and motorists to a stony track which itself merged into Coker's deeply-rutted lane. Coker and his brawny sons encouraged weeds to clog the footpath sign at the gate. They could have taken it down with impunity but this would have denied them the satisfaction of mischief. Many of Uncle Ben's contemporaries, including the Cokers, needed props for their self-assertion.

Uncle Ben wasn't particularly friendly with the Cokers. No-one was. I remembered as a snotty-nosed mudlark being discovered bird-nesting in Coker's Wood by old man Coker – then, I suppose, about sixty – who parted the branches of a hazel bush and stood in cruciform silhouette saying nothing while his dogs ran rings around me. I used to see him strolling aimlessly across his land in the gloaming, his path signalled by the flaring ember of a cigarette. But now he was old and sick and reduced to lifeless supervision of his three sons, two of whom had acquired his sourness. They would have been toddlers when Bruno and company visited the farm, just like me, open to everything but blind to its significance. In the constant motion of their industry, with their father occupying rather than holding its centre on a rickety stool, they were a walking vindication of their custom against our ambition. Uncle Ben said of old man Coker that he'd put the 'cant' in 'cantankerous'.

The Cokers knew why Uncle Ben had come and nodded when he pointed to the paddock beside the farmhouse. It held an old mare, which pulled the Cokers' cart about the lanes, and a doleful mule. There had once been another horse, the mule's more majestic parent; and a donkey, its awkward, submissive mother.

Uncle Ben rested a foot on the gate and tapped his pipe.

'One Christmas,' he said, 'that mule's father was choking on its umbilical cord. Bruno knew he was on the way. They wanted to call the vet but Bruno said he could do it. And he did – with some rope and a lot of Italian know-how. Then he went, just like that.'

'The horse?'

'No, Bruno, yer daft bugger! With the others, on a lorry. The war was over, you see.'

I felt that these were disclosures not being made lightly. How many had seen Bruno's drawings or even knew they existed? Uncle Ben had a small collection of books, limited yet suited to the purpose of confirming the rumbling of other worlds.

'The horse, too,' he said. 'But not before it had had its way with Coker's donkey. There's the result. Sterile issue.' He indicated the mule with his wet pipe-stem.

During my second year at college, Uncle Ben wrote to say that old man Coker had died and that the boys were selling up to go in for a bigger place. There was to be an auction of machinery and stock. He hoped to buy the mule, as one of the boys had 'given me the nod'.

I suppose I got home once a term. Neither my parents nor Uncle Ben had a phone then. Letters were vehicles of quiet dissemination in which one received postal orders and inklings of things going awry. 'Your uncle has ripped up his beautiful garden and is sowing grass seed,' my mother wrote. 'Whatever for we can't imagine. He's never been forthcoming.' This last sentence was meant to suggest a new, immediate concern but it might as well have summarised a lifetime's futile attempts at union. Surrounded by married relatives with children, Uncle Ben's bachelorhood seemed like a redoubt, a social position felt to be wanting. These things must also have had their unfathomable reaches.

He bought the mule. The new farm owners turned the building into a home and rented out the fields as pasture. I suppose they were among the first of a wave of the immigrant rich. For a time the mule was kept in a field on a neighbouring farm, but Uncle Ben fell out with the farmer over something trivial and withdrew the animal to his back 'lawn': a quarter-acre by now sweet with clover and grass a foot high. Here it remained, except when Uncle Ben trailed it round the village, its reluctance to be exercised a caricature of beastly stubbornness. This was a year after I failed my exams. One evening, out of work and out of favour, I stood with Uncle Ben in his back garden, staring at the mule and its sad, drooping features.

Then Uncle Ben began to neglect himself. He refused to eat properly and he was allowing the house to crumble around him. Protests and offers of help were unavailing. I saw that the settee was riddled with tiny holes made by showering tobacco ash. He built a manger for the mule, complete with chimney stack and lean-to. He became very silent. One of the first calls on my parents' new phone was from one of his neighbours. 'You'd better come round,' he said. 'It's mad. What he's doing is mad.'

The PoWs' birches were growing tall and slender. As our car turned the corner at the old toll house, they came into view, swaying in the headlights like phantom dancers, the council houses plan having been shelved.

A group of people were outside the gate. There was a fire at the back. 'He's locked himself in,' said the man who'd phoned. I went to the window. I could make out Uncle Ben in shadow on the settee, like Old Coker that time in the wood, and behind him, at the bottom of the garden, the manger in flames. I waved, but I must have appeared to him as he appeared to me, a figure with its features removed, a half-obliterated presence of something that might have been, now reduced to gesture. They found the mule on Forestry Commission land among the dull pines, staring in the wet at the dead end of its existence.

Uncle Ben was sent to Ashbourne Court, the place every pestered mother threatened her kids with on the grounds that her committal would be to their detriment through the pain of guilt and separation. He spent three years at 'the Ash' before he died. I don't think he said a word during that whole time, but we visited just the same. Friendly doctors would explain to us what was going on in his head, as though we were ignorant people who had taken on more than we could properly handle. They sat between us on the park benches, daring the mute Uncle Ben to contradict them. Then they'd leave him with a pat on the back. These visits eventually tired the others and, in the end, I was the only one who made the weekly trip. During summer I would wait and they would bring him to me; in winter I'd be led straight to his ward. At first I believed that his natural reticence had simply become pathological and once or twice I thought of telling the doctors in the hope that the theory might be useful to them in devising therapy. Then I had the idea that Uncle Ben could really understand everything, that he could soak up sights and sounds without, at last, the need to react. These were not enlightened days at 'the Ash'; they were days of interrupted peace, of distant skirmishes in corridors and the foetal position assumed unnoticed among the rosebeds. In Uncle Ben's case the haven could stand it. I reached the stage where I could tell him what I'd made of things so far and how a setback need not necessarily make you cower before the seemingly impossible. In one sense I was defying him to accept that my confessions were an adjunct of post-war privilege; in another I was goading him into speech, but his face remained almost beatific, his tongue motionless. I convinced myself that these were thoughts that Uncle Ben shared but which had always had to scramble up the rock face of his obtuseness. Yet not even the possibility of a mind in retreat from light and purpose could advance my unburdening to its extremity. I realised that important matters had once wedged themselves into his life. But they had departed, leaving a door banging uselessly in an empty room.

When we collected his belongings, I knew we would be travelling light on our return. His bed was already being made for its next occupant. In the room, there was a sense of someone who had passed through, having been no trouble yet having missed out on so much.

Acknowledgements

Thanks are due to the editors of the following publications in which most of these stories, or early versions of them, first appeared: *London Magazine*, *Staple*, *Panurge*, *Sons of Camus Writers International Journal*, *Brand*, *Dreamcatcher* and *Black Mountain Review* (Ulster). Special thanks to David Caddy, editor of *Tears in the Fence*, for publishing so many of the stories that didn't make this list. No one should forget the modest renaissance of the short story in Wales instigated in the 1980s by Arthur Smith, editor of *Cambrensis*, who started me off.

I would also like to thank the writer Richard (Lewis) Davies, founder of Parthian, for his commitment to Anglo-Welsh short fiction and his willingness to allow me to make some small contribution to it; and Eluned Gramich, my editor, for reading the manuscript so assiduously and making the improvements demanded by sense, shape and structure.

'Nomad' was anthologised in *Mother's Baby, Papa's Maybe* (Parthian/Arts Council of Wales/Cambrensis) and 'The Lister Building' in *Signals 2* (London Magazine Editions).

'Mrs Kuroda on Penyfan' won the Rhys Davies Prize for short fiction.

PARTHIAN

Award-winning
Welsh Writing

www.parthianbooks.co.uk